Ghost Dater
brandi autumn

For every woman who has ever dated a man.
This one's for you.

"A MALE BODY WAS found in Buffalo Bayou this morning. This is the second body found this month. Authorities are working to identify both bodies and if there is a link between the two. Due to the unusual amount of rain Houston has received lately, the bodies could have been in the bayou for months..."

The video zooms out, showing the overflowing bayou. Text in white bold letters over the running news video states: IS A WOMAN LEADING MEN INTO THE WATER TO THEIR DEMISE IN THE BAYOU?!

2.4 million views; 244.6k likes; 3k saves; 20.9k comments
Comments:
Ivy's Momma: Did they tell her "no"?
Scarlet: Why didn't they fight back? And why was he out so late?
Luna Bella: A false claim like that could ruin her life.
Neon Whisper: What was he wearing?

Transplant Knight: Did he say clearly he did not consent to drowning?

Meghan Sparkles: Did they try saying no?

Navaeh: Why weren't they watching their drinks?

Obsidian Soul: Why was he out at night?

MarieMarie: I'm sure she wouldn't do that, she has a father, brother, a son...

Jo Chronicles: Did he just lie there and act like he wanted it?

Rogue Aria: What did he do to trigger her?

Maya Moonlight: Why would they even go near a woman they didn't know? ?

Shade of Dark: We need to hear both sides of the story.

KC Creates: How do we know they weren't teasing her with talk of wanting a late night swim?

Sofia: Where was their taser, pepper spray, keys between fingers, and cup cover?

Shadow Readers: I can't believe he was so irresponsible.

Madison

GLANCING IN THE MIRROR, one last time, I check my reflection, wiping away the mascara from under my eyes and smoothing down my hair — a pang of nervousness hits me, but it's now or never.

Beep. Beep. Beep.

"Hate the dating apps? Then let me get on them for you! Hi, I'm Madison and I want to date for you. How will that work? I will get on the dating apps for you, I will create your profile, and do all the swiping as you, for you. I screen the men before passing only the good ones to you to meet. Message me to get started! Also, it's my birthday, so show me some love!"

I press the red button again to stop the recording. The video immediately plays back. I cringe hearing my voice; seriously if I sound like that, I feel sorry for everyone I talk to. I watch myself in the video point at the camera right on cue, and blow a kiss at the end. After watching it back three times, I realize I shouldn't have done all that; but this video will have to do, I don't want to rerecord. This is the first time I'm putting this kind of thing out into the dark void of the web to see if it is something someone wants.

I caption the post "DM me to help you find your soulmate! #dating #single #letmehelpyou #matchmaker"

Should I put more hashtags to get more reach? Do people still search by hashtags? I use social media daily, but somehow still don't know exactly how it all works. Will anyone even see this video anyway? Will anyone put their faith in me and have me date for them to find their match? I guess I will find out — *I can't believe I am doing this.*

Just post it, Madison, I tell myself; just see what happens. I press the post button at the bottom of the screen. A loading counter pops up: 60%...72%...94%...100%. The video pops up on my screen one more time; I watch it before silencing my phone.

Whatever happens, happens. I am not going to look at it again today, or I will drive myself crazy worrying about how many people are viewing it and what response it is getting. Anyway, it's time to head into the office.

"GIRL!" I LOOK UP; Robbie is making a beeline for my cubicle, yelling from across the office. Rolling my eyes at his dramatics, a small smile tugs at my lips, because I do love his dramatics all the same. I still look around to make sure no one is looking our way — I hate drawing attention to myself.

"I saw the video you posted this morning!" He holds up his phone, as if I don't know what video he is talking about. My face frozen on his screen, mouth half-open, eyes half-shut—every feature slightly wrong, every angle unkind.

"What video?" Lauri stands up from her cubicle that is close to mine.

"Oh nothing," I say; I can feel my face growing hotter by the second.

"Apparently, our very own Madi is a modern-day matchmaker!" Robbie says and I wince hearing him call me Madi. I shrug, wishing he wasn't doing this right now, or ever. He plays the video for Lauri to see.

"Just something I thought about trying out. I've helped a few friends find their significant others. It's stupid." I shrug it again and tug at my bright red ear, as if that will stop the embarrassment.

"That's actually genius, Madison! I heard those dating apps are brutal." Lauri sits back down at her desk; our cubicle walls don't go all the way up — the whole open floor plan movement hit our office a few years back — so I can still see her.

"Cam and I always say how lucky we are that we met before having to get on those." She turns back to her computer; I assume to get back to work. I need to do the same.

"She is right, Madi." Ugh. "It really is genius. And this video already has five thousand views!" Robbie hangs his arms over the side of my cubicle.

I put my fingers, dry with chipped, pink polish, back on the keyboard trying to finish the email I was typing out, but I suddenly cannot remember what I was going to type — 5,000 views? Has the video really already been watched that many times?

"How does it work?" Robbie asks, not ready to end the conversation.

I look up at him confused for a second before realizing he means the matchmaking, but I don't want to continue talking about it. Robbie and Lauri are my work friends, but I still keep my personal life as private as I can. I didn't even realize he was following me on any of my social media accounts — I make a mental note to block him later.

"Better question is, what are we doing for lunch?" I deflect perfectly.

"Madi, I'm not sure why you are like this. Childhood trauma I suppose," he rolls his eyes. "I mean, we all have them. But you are going to have to let people in. And now, you've exposed yourself on a platform with millions of people. People are going to see you." I take a deep breath — he's right, seriously, what was I thinking?!

Lauri ignores him. "Let's go to that juice and salad place," she says, not looking up from her computer. We can always count on Lauri to make the executive decisions about lunch. Robbie and I will go back and forth for hours trying to decide, but not Lauri — she just picks a place with no debate about it.

"And cake!" Robbie adds, Lauri finally looks up, puzzled. "For Madi's birthday?"

"Oh, I am the worst! Happy Birthday, Madison!" She says with a strained smile, clearly frustrated with herself for forgetting the date.

"Thanks. And it's not big deal. No cake needed."

As Robbie opens his mouth to protest, I put my hand up and he closes it without uttering another word. After staring at me for another solid minute, he whispers 'happy birthday' and sulks back to his office. Lauri and I are stuck in open cubicles in the middle of the office floor, while

Robbie gets a door he can close with a nice view of downtown.

"Well, what did you expect would happen?" Ellie, my best friend from college, video called me as soon as she got off work.

"I don't know? Not this." I get comfortable on my bed. "I mean I thought the same 500 people who normally see my videos would see it and I'd get like one or two of those people interested. Definitely not all this!"

"Yes, but think about it. There's a reason you wanted to do this for people. Those apps suck! Everyone feels the same, and you would be relieving women of this burden."

"You are...right," I barely answer, as I am also reading through the first direct message I received—there are about 82 messages.

"What's going on?" Ellie asks, noticing I was distracted.

"Huh?" I click back so her face fills my screen.

"You look upset or disturbed." I can never hide my feelings because my facial expressions—they give me away every time.

"Why are people so weird and awful?" I click to my direct messages. "This man sent me a message berating me, calling me nasty names, and then asking me to do all kinds of gross sexual activities on him."

"Gross. I bet you are going to get a lot of those."

I hesitantly click on the next message.

> Hi! I randomly found your video, the universe knows I am struggling! Or it's the algorithm. Either way, here you are and here I am. I don't know how much to include here but I would really love your help! Can you message me back with details of exactly what this entails? I am so tired of scrolling and ending up with trolls or ghosted. This is a serious inquiry. I will pay you. Hope to hear from you soon. Kisses, Layla.

"What are you going to do, Madison?" Robbie is the only person, besides my dad to call me Madi—everyone else knows how much I hate it. Robbie knows how much I hate it, but he still uses it every time, anyway.

"About what? The troll? Oh, nothing. I deleted that message."

"No, this whole thing."

"I guess I'm going to help her."

"Her? Her who?" I realize she didn't read the same message I just did.

"The first message I got seriously asking for help. I'll start there. Help as many women as I can, or try to. I don't know, is this crazy?"

"No, this is great. Let's talk money. How much are you going to charge for your services?" Ellie, always the businesswoman.

We met in business school, and I always knew she was destined for great things: CFO, top 40 under 40, or something like that. I was just there because it seemed more lucrative than an art degree and easier than a science degree. I also could never reconcile those two interests; art and science don't really go together.

"I will put together a price list for you." I see her grab her computer and know I will receive a detailed spreadsheet soon. She starts talking about income and expenses; I tune her out. She types away while I think about how to respond to Layla's message.

"Alright, I just shared a spreadsheet with you," Ellie says. Sure enough, in my email inbox is a spreadsheet titled 'Ghost Dater.'

"Ohmygosh, Ellie! First, thank you for putting this together. But ghost dater?" She winces as if she has done something wrong. "That's genius! I have been wondering what I should call this. I love it!"

"See I can get a little creative sometimes," she beams.

"I'm a ghost dater." I smile, a real, genuine smile.

The document has a three-tier plan with various pricing, potential expenses to be incurred, and a place for a client list and notes. It is color-coded to perfection.

"So, I am going to do this, huh?" I ask as I type in Layla on tab labeled 'client list.'

"Hell yea you are!" Ellie, always my cheerleader. "Listen, Madison, you are amazing at reading people and you've now set up three couples. Just try this and see how it goes."

"You are right. Just look at you and Nick."

"Speaking of, he just got home. I'll talk to you later."

I yell to Nick, saying hello. We say our goodbyes and I love yous. I lay back on my bed, recalling the night I met Nick.

"Hi, I'm Madison." I said, jutting out my hand for the stranger to shake.

"Uh...oh. Hi." He hesitates but takes my hand—I'm surprised how strong he grips my hand, especially considering how taken aback he is by my introduction.

"I'm Nick."

By the end of our 15 minute conversation, I knew his major, future career goals, family history, and how he ended up at the University of Kentucky.

"Tell me, Nick. Are you single?"

He rubs the back of his neck, nervously. "Uh, I'm sorry. I just don't...you're not...listen. I liked talking with..."

I put my hand up and laughed. "Oh! Not for me. I'm not asking for me. You seem like a great guy but for my best friend."

His shoulders relax and I don't know if I should be offended. "Oh!"

"I guess that might sound strange, just after talking to you, I think you and her would be great together. So are you single?"

"Yes, I am. So you are here being her wing-woman? Do you guys do this often?"

I start to reach out and touch his arm while laughing again, but I retreat before making contact. "No, no, Nick. I swear, I've never done this before, but as I got to know you, I realized you would be great for her. Here," I pull my phone out of my handbag. "Let me show you her picture."

He put his hands up. "Actually, can you first tell me about her and why think we would be a great match? Is she here tonight?" He starts looking around the bar, wondering which woman was Ellie.

I told Nick about how Ellie is the sweetest, most caring, and thoughtful person I have ever met. I only gave him a brief overview of her family, what she is studying, but I told him she could go into more details because that's her story to tell. After hearing all I had to say, Nick agreed to meet Ellie.

"She was here, but went home a little earlier to study for an exam she has tomorrow. Can I get your number to pass along to her?" I handed him my phone to create a new contact before he could respond.

I practically ran home to my shared apartment with Ellie to tell her I had met her future husband. She also thought I was crazy.

"I swear! Ellie! I found you husband. I can feel it in my bones." Before she could protest, I told her everything Nick had told me about himself and a picture I creepily took of him across the room.

"See! He's great and perfect for you."

"I don't know, Madison. This is weird. I wasn't even there."

I poured us each a glass of wine—I don't drink much, the combination between alcohol and medicine don't bode well for me, but it felt necessary for this conversation. By the time we finished the bottle, Ellie had agreed to text Nick to set up a date—it took her another week to actually message him.

Ellie and Nick dated the rest of our college years, moved into an apartment together after graduation, got married a few years ago, have a toddler, and are currently pregnant with their second child.

My first matchmaking success story. I hope to add to my resume. I double check my messages—Layla hasn't messaged me back yet.

Detective Oliver

"Good morning, Liam." I say setting down the extra coffee I grabbed on my way into work this morning. He had texted saying he got called in around four in the morning. Being the rookie on the team, he is on call 24/7. It might have been eight years ago for me, but I remember how awful and long the nights can be.

"Detective," Liam nods in my direction, saying both hello and thank you without even looking my way.

"What did you get called in for?" I can tell he's busy—I assume writing the report from the call—but I still bug him about it anyway. He looks up, sighs loudly, and finally grabs the coffee.

He's got it much easier being a rookie these days than I had it. He only gets called in on real calls; I got prank calls from the other detectives at all times of the night. They claimed they had it worse than that in their time. With each new generation of detectives, the bullying gets less and less severe.

"Just a car on fire." He downs about half the coffee in one gulp.

"Anyone inside?"

He shakes his head. "They thought so, but thankfully, no. Could you imagine? That would have been a nightmare." I don't need to imagine—I've seen a few bodies burned up in car fires.

"Lucky you," I tease, grinning as I walk to my office. The only way to get through this type of work is to make jokes. At least that's the way I get through this type of work.

I sit down at my desk, turn on my computer and enter the password—just as I do every morning. The coffee cup sits in the middle of the coaster, three black pens in the small holder on the right corner of the desk, a spiral planner already opened to today's date, and a to-do list spelled out hour by hour.

"Detective Oliver," Joe bursts into my office.

"What's up, Chief?"

"A body was found."

"I know, Joe. I got the file from Detective Casey yesterday." The case file showed up on my desk yesterday, I didn't ask any questions, just dove right in.

"They are already reporting on it, even though we asked them not to." I roll my eyes—the media never listens to us; they just want the breaking, shocking story first.

I look down at my calendar. "I am interviewing the man who discovered the body at 10."

"This is the first body we have found in the bayou in a few years," Joe reminds me.

"I understand, sir," I say, holding back a sigh. "Liam and I will be working to identify the body as quickly as we can."

He pauses while nodding his head, stares off in thought, then turns to walk out of my office.

"Hey, Joe?" I stop him.

He turns back around, but doesn't say anything. I bite the inside of my cheek.

"Did you ever have a case that just ate at you?"

"Of course. A few."

"Did you solve them all?"

When I flipped open the case file, I was expecting the usual: timestamps, photos, inconsistencies I can tug apart. The first page gave me nothing but a prickle at the back of my neck. Each line feels like it's hiding something, as if the truth slipped between the margins. By the time I reach the last paragraph, a thought has already rooted itself: this case won't give up its truth easily...maybe not at all.

He shakes his head. "Not all of them, no."

"How do you deal with that?" I have had a few cases that I wasn't able to tie up neatly with a bow, but none of them pulled at me this much.

"Even Kobe Bryant missed 50% of the shots he took."

I stifle a laugh—Joe loves to make basketball references, that I never really understand. "Well, good thing Kobe wasn't investigating murders."

He chuckles and walks out of my office. Liam slides in the door, as if he was just waiting for Joe to leave before he did so.

"He seems, I don't know?" Liam questions.

"He wants this solved quickly. Cases like these are always sensationalized by the media and bring a lot of attention."

"And fear, I suppose." Liam shrugs.

Joe was generous when he said a "body" was found. An arm attached to half a torso was pulled from the bayou. I do not want to know what is running in those waters to cause that kind of damage.

"Does it get easier?" Liam asked when we were at the scene. It doesn't, really—it never gets easier.

"He's here." Liam knocks on my open door. I look down at the clock on the computer; right on time.

"Hi." I give the man sitting in the interrogation room a weak smile. "My name is Detective Oliver."

He stands, shoulders hunched, making him seem much smaller than he actually is. He takes my hand to shake, but says nothing.

"Andy, right?"

"Andy Mastrason." He is soft spoken, I can hardly hear him.

"Andy, it's nice to meet you. I'm sorry it's under these circumstances." He stares straight through me, knowing our paths would never cross otherwise. "Can you tell me what happened? Also, this interview is being recorded. I know you signed the consent, I just wanted to make it known as well."

"Yes," his voice is shaky. "I was," he pauses. "I was walking along the bayou and saw something in the water." He pauses again.

"Take your time," I tap my pen while trying to be empathetic. I should have sent Liam to talk to him. "The Buffalo Bayou, right?"

"Yes. The Buffalo Bayou."

I nod for him to continue.

"When I got closer, it took me a minute. But I realized it was a human arm sticking out of the water. At first, I thought it was fake," his breath increases. "So I grabbed it. I thought it was fake, like a mannequin or something. Oh God. I pulled it out of the water. It wasn't fake. It was real. It wasn't fake." A scream erupts from the depths of his body.

"Andy, Andy. It's okay." I try calming him. Seeing a dead body is jarring, shocking, gruesome, and like I told Liam, it never gets easier—even after all these years.

Liam walks in the room bringing Andy some water. His breathing finally normalizing.

Andy drinks the water and asks, "Am I in trouble?"

"No sir. We just need to know all the details that led to you discovering the body. Any information you may have can help us with identifying the person and what happened."

Liam is better at talking with people; he really understand the psychology of how to communicate to get people to open up. I am better at finding and following the hard facts without the emotions humans may have. Liam stays in the room, but doesn't say anymore.

"What were you doing walking along the Bayou yesterday afternoon?" This isn't a great question—there's a paved trail running along both sides of the bayou for pedestrian any time of day.

"I like to take a walk every day after I eat lunch, between jobs."

"What's your job?"

"I'm a plumber."

"What did you do after you pulled the body from the water?" I can see his eyes flash back to that moment again, secretly hoping he doesn't start screaming again.

"Well, I screamed. I'm sorry about screaming. I just..."

"It's okay," I say.

"Then I called 9-1-1."

Andy tells us he hadn't noticed any unusual activity along the bayou during the time he is there daily. He said the water had been unusually high, due to lots of rain Houston has been having, so it's been full and rushing quickly a lot. However, he saw nothing of significance leading up the discovery he made. And since there wasn't much of a body, there wasn't much identifying features for him to tell us if he had seen the man also walking the bayou.

"Thank you, Andy. You've been a great help." Liam and I walk out of the room; I signal to the officer outside the room to escort Andy out of the building.

"Do you think he has anything to do with this?" Liam asks.

"Doubt it." I shake my head.

Normally, it takes a few weeks for the medical examiner to look at the body and write up her report. Thankfully, she hasn't had a body come through her office in a few days and has a new assistant to help when it does get backlogged.

"Ash!" I say as I walk into her office.

Ashley and I went to high school together. I never would have thought we would end up working together all these years later. Ash, with her long blond hair, always pulled in a bun, dainty frame and bubbly personality, filled all of the high school stereotypes. She was head cheerleader, captain of the volleyball team, and dated the quarterback.

"Grace!" She gives me a hug. "I was hoping this would be your case."

I smile. "You just knew I'd love a dismembered body, huh?"

She nods and walks over to the table where said body was laid out.

"Did you just finish? I can come back if not."

"Please, stay. I'm wrapping up, here. They just phoned to tell me the detective on the case was headed over, so I got him out so you could have a look too."

"They didn't tell you it was me?"

She shakes her head. "They are still giving me a hard time. Wanted me to sweat, waiting to see who was working this one. They made me think it was Detective Casey."

I shake my head. "You've been here over a year! You'd think they would get over it by now." She shrugs and I add, "You don't like Detective Casey?"

"Oh no, I do. That's the problem." She laughs.

I learned through social media, after getting her biology degree, she moved back to the Houston suburb we grew up in and started working at the local funeral home—as a receptionist at first. Eventually, she asked to work with the bodies. After learning all she could about preserving the body after it dies, she went back to school to learn about why it dies. It's such a small world that she would end up as the medical examiner for Harris County Sheriff's Office and the examiner I would work with most often.

We both roll our eyes and she motions for me to get closer to the body. "Look at this."

"What do you think caused the dismemberment? An animal? Or a person, before it went into the water?"

She shakes her head. "I'm not sure completely, but it doesn't appear he went in the water like this."

"He?"

"Yes. We will try our best for time of death. Bodies don't normally stay in the water that long before being found."

"So are you saying he didn't go into the bayou recently?"

"Weeks to a month or more."

"Hm. Can you let me know what you find out about this one?" I say this every time, even though no matter what she finds out, she will let me know, it's her job after all—she still nods.

"Hey, Grace?"

I turn back to her.

"You want to go get that drink or coffee with me?" She has been begging me to go out with her since she started working here. We were close the first few years of high school—I fit some of those same stereotypes she did. Minus the long blond hair, I was a cheerleader, I played volleyball, and dated a football player. We were inseparable, until the last few months of senior year.

"We will, Ash. One day. Can't today though. Sorry." I offer a weak apology. She shrugs and smiles. I walk out before she can suggest another day to get together and find a toilet to throw up in. It doesn't get easier seeing bodies in that manner, but I haven't thrown up leaving the medical examiner's office in years.

"YOU HAVEN'T BEEN HOME this late in a long time," James greets me at the door like he does every night. He takes my bag, putting it on a hook—my hook—by the door.

I sigh. "I know." I sigh again, as I am taking off my shoes, lining them up next to James's black loafers. It took 34 years, but I was lucky enough to find someone as obsessive about being tidy as I am.

James walks back to the kitchen, I follow.

"Dinner is almost ready." He says as he pours me a glass of white wine and tops off his glass.

"Bless you," I say as I bring the wine first to my nose—breathing in the alcohol before a drop hits my lips.

He finishes plating the meal and puts them on the table in the kitchen; I grab forks and napkins, trying to do my part.

"How was class? " I ask as he takes his first bite.

"Rrrr," he tries to speak with his mouth full. We both laugh and he raises one finger up, signaling to give him a moment.

I take a bite, a much smaller bite than my husband, finishing chewing and am able to speak before he can. "Wow, babe! This is really good!" When he set the plate down, it's contents didn't look like anything we had before, but I am used to James experimenting in the kitchen.

He nods his head. "It's a new recipe I found and I got the fish from a local market instead of the store, so it should be fresh."

"I can tell. It tastes so fresh." I shove more in my mouth, more haphazardly than before.

"Oh, class was good. The usual." We eat in silence for a few moments, savoring the meal and marinating on our day.

James finally says, "I have papers to read tonight."

I nod; James always brings home papers to read and grade, as a tenured professor at University of Houston teaching mostly Freshman Composition.

"What was the assignment this time?"

"Fifteen hundred word review of a meal you had without mentioning the exact food."

"Interesting." He always comes up with unique writing assignments that really challenge his students use of words.

When I was a freshman taking my writing class, it was the last thing I wanted to do. Then, I grew up, and now 90% of my job is writing. No wonder all students are required to take it in high school and university.

"Fifteen hundred words seems like a lot for a food review."

James finishes his bite. "It's just enough. You know that most people describe things, especially food, with minimal uninspiring words like good or bad." He rolls his eyes—James hardly ever rolls his eyes.

"You're right. You always have such great writing prompts." I say, staring into the emptiness of my once white plate.

"How was it?" James touches my shoulder.

"Huh?"

"Everything okay?"

"Oh, yea. What did you ask before?" I move to stand.

"I just asked how your food was?"

"Good." We bust out laughing.

"You sure you okay? You kind of disappeared there." I nod and he kisses my forehead.

I start cleaning up the dishes while James goes to his grading; this is the arrangement we have—he cooks, I clean. However, I got the better end of the bargain because James is a clean cook and I generally only have to clean our plates and utensils.

"Any of these good?" I ask picking up a couple of papers James threw on the floor next to where he is sitting.

He motions for me to join him in the over sized chair. "A couple." He hands me the one he was reading.

The liquid burst in my mouth as my teeth cut through outer shell. I swirl it with my tongue, slightly burning it.

I look at James, raising my eyebrow; he simply nods. I don't keep reading through; I lay my head on his shoulder. He finishes reading the paper in his hands, marks it with a B and tosses it on the floor. My adorable, clean freak husband always makes a mess when grading papers—I will never understand it.

"What's on that beautiful brain of yours?" He rubs his right hand on my head, kissing my forehead. I look up at him and sigh.

"Oh, it's just this case. Something is going on. I can feel it."

"What do you feel?"

I shrug. "I don't know. I just got a feeling."

"You think there's more bodies in that water?"

I smile at him; James always takes interest and listens when I talk, even though I know he hates it. James could go the rest of his life not hearing about another crime.

I shrug, again. "I'm just telling you, it's something." I touch my stomach. What is it they say about trusting a woman's intuition?

"I am sure you are right, you normally are." He leans down and kisses my forehead again. "Why is this case bothering you so much? I know you care about every case you work, but you seem extra stressed about this one."

I shake my head and lay back on this chest. "Again, I just don't know."

I've worked many homicide cases throughout my career and I always bring my work home; the worries, the anxieties, the fears, the questions. However, I am generally able to switch it off after a little while at home. This case though, it has been staying with me—keeping me up at night.

James shifts in the seat, dumping me as he stands. "Where are you going?" I whine, wanting to stay in his arms the rest of the night.

"I'll be right back." He disappears into the kitchen again—I can't see him from where I am sitting in the living room. We bought this old home last year; it's so old, that every room is segregated from the others; not an open floor plan like most new homes. Plans to renovate are stuffed in a drawer in the office desk—drawn up by an architect.

Something always comes up preventing us from starting on any of the projects.

James is right back, carrying a small tray. He puts it on the coffee table next to me. A cup of hot tea, three frozen cookie dough bites, and a mint laid out perfectly. Whenever I struggle sleeping, or have a rough day, these little things James does make it better. I pull the cup up to my mouth, the steam filling my nose. The chamomile relaxes the tension in my shoulders, but not the biting feeling in my gut.

Madison

Beep. Beep. Beep.

"Hi guys! I didn't think my last video would get so much attention! And I am slowly going to answer as many messages as I can. First things first, if you would like my services, private message me and I will get to it as soon as I can! Basically, how it works, since many are asking, I take on your identity for the dating apps. We talk and possibly meet in person if you are local, so I can get an idea of your personality and what you like and want out of the dating experience. Then, I do all the hard work for you. I'll swipe and vet the man or men and have initial conversations. Once I get a good sense of the men, I'll pass on the candidates I think will be a good match. Also, sorry men! I can only do this for the ladies, since I am one, obviously. And no, I will not meet any of the men in person, so I will not be falling in love with any of them. I am strictly in this to help other women, not myself. Yes, there is a fee for my

services, you can find all that information linked on my bio. Let me see, I think that's it. I have a lot of messages already, so please be patient." #dating #ghostdater

92.1k views; 35.9k likes; 192 saves; 340 comments

Comments:

Rose Quartz Dream: Seriously, you are doing amazing work!

*MidnightCipher: Please answer my DM. Trying to be patient. *grimacing emoji***

Iron Wolf: You are crazy woman.

ZekeVolt: Catfishing is now being praised? What next?!

Roxy Reign: Love this!

Sofia Sparks: Are you going to be showing us your process?

Logan435: This is false. Don't believe this dumb, fat bitch.

Indie_Atlas88: Thank you, girl for doing this for other women.

Ziggy_Toast: Can't stand being on these apps, would love someone to do the work for me.

Carol209: Just about the delete these apps too. Need your help.

Momma_Elliex2: Love you girl!

I close the application—I shouldn't read the comments on these videos I post. People can be so cruel. Instead, I dial Layla's number she provided to me in a private message. I told her I would video call her today to get started with the process of finding her a man to date.

"Hello! It's great to meet you. I'm Madison." I start talking as soon as she answers the call.

"Hi! You have no idea, I'm so glad you actually messaged me back. I feel like I won the lottery!"

"Where do you live?" I ask.

"Oh. I'm in the medical center area-ish." Layla answers as a small, white dog jumps into the view.

"He, or she, is so cute! I didn't know you had a dog. I am adding that to your profile. Any other pets?"

She makes the dog lay down next to her. "Just this one. Her name is Joy and she is six years old."

I write down 'must love dogs' in my notebook. I am taking as many notes on Layla as I can. I was able to get some information from her social media accounts already.

"I am close to the med center, too." I lie. "Would you be interested in meeting somewhere? It might be a little easier to get to know you in person."

Layla agrees and sends me the location of a bar close to her house. I tell her I need an hour to get ready, but really it's going to take me about that long to get to her side of town from where I actually live.

Even my coworkers I've known for eight years don't know I live on the outskirts of Houston. I hate I cannot afford a decent apartment in the city, even with my good job. The only thing I ever wanted since I moved to the fourth largest city was to live in the heart of the chaos, right where the city breathes the loudest. But moving here alone after college—young and broke—I couldn't afford it. Even through my salary has increased over the years, so has the cost of living.

LAYLA, 29, NURSE, HOUSTON
BIO: Compassionate caregiver by day, adventure seeker by night! When I'm not busy saving lives, you can find me curled up with a good book, running the trails, or brunch on a dog-friendly patio. I value honesty, kindness, and a good sense of humor. Looking for someone who shares my zest for life and is ready to embark on this crazy journey of life.
Looking for long-term relationship
5'4"
Grad school degree
No kids, but wants
Spiritual
From Houston, Texas
Interests: Running, Reading, Visual Arts, Restaurants, Dogs, Brunch, Music

I activated Layla's dating profile at nine last night; it's only six in the morning and she already has 53 likes on her profile. I know a lot of men just swipe right on every woman on these dating applications, but I have a good feeling about this and finding someone for Layla. I expected a lot of likes as soon as I posted it. We picked out some great photos for her profile that show not only her beauty but also her personality. Of course, we included a great photo of her with her dog.

I annoyingly asked her how it was possible someone like her is still single. I know single people get that question a lot and the only logical answer is that they haven't met their person.

She had shrugged and said, "I was in a serious relationship for a long time and since then I just haven't found someone I really wanted to be with. Maybe my standards are too high?"

"No, no." I shook my head. "Your standards should be high! Don't ever settle just to have someone. Plus, you are a great catch. You are stunning, you have your shit together, a great career, you want to marriage and kids. It's...these men out here or should I say boys." She nodded, understandingly, tucking a short, dark brown ringlet behind her left ear.

Layla has an infectious personality, she is quiet, but after only one meeting I know she has a kind soul. She has a warmth that's steady, calm, and deeply attentive. There's a light in her eyes, hopeful, and empathy that runs deep.

I only have ten minutes before I have to get ready for work, but I click on the first match.

Kory, 31, Engineer, Houston
Bio: Just ask

"Ugh. Kory, not starting out strong." I say, aloud, to no one. "But this first picture is cute." I keep scrolling.

Quote I live by: "Live everyday as if it's your last."

"Okay, but do you really, Kory?"
The next picture is of him holding a fish he presumably caught. Immediate swipe left. I don't know why men think pictures with dead animals are the way to a woman's heart—even if she likes to fish, like I do, I don't want to see you holding a dead animal on your dating profile. I should confirm with Layla that she feels the same—I have to remind myself I'm her, here.

The next match pops up.

Victor, 26, Medical Sales, Houston

No bio, no pictures. Swipe left. Why publish an account if you aren't finished with it? Ugh. I cannot do this right now. I need to set some dedicated time to parse through these profiles. Good thing Ellie insisted I charge money for this—it's going to be a second full-time job.

"MADI, CALL ME BACK. This is your dad."

I stare at the transcript of the voicemail I didn't listen to. It has been three days and I still have yet to call him back. I know exactly how the conversation will go. Well, it could go one of two ways; either he will ask me to send him money or he will tell me to come back home—it's laughable calling that place "home."

Please don't answer, please don't answer, please don't answer, I plead during the three rings on the other end of the phone.

"Hey...dad," I say hesitantly.

"Pumpkin!" He exclaims, like he is actually happy to hear from me—at least he seems like he's in a good mood today. Maybe he hasn't had a drink today, or maybe he has. It's gotten more difficult figuring out if the alcohol makes him nicer or not. When I was younger, it seemed to put him in a good mood, like it opened up something inside him that could be happy, playful, excited to have a child around. At some point, things shifted and it just made him more angry, more aggressive.

"Is everything okay?"

"Took you long enough to call me back." There went his good mood. "What if something was wrong?!"

"What do you want dad?" My jaw tightens.

"I need you to come home."

I pinch the bridge of my nose between my thumb and forefinger. "Why dad?" I don't want to hear his reason, nor will it sway me to go back to Utah for any amount of time. I have only been back there once since leaving after graduating high school.

"It's your uncle. He isn't doing well. It's Emmett."

I pull the phone away from my mouth so he can't hear me sigh. "Emmett has been dead for like five years. And how would me coming home help Bill?"

"When did you get so cold, Madi?" I roll my eyes. "You were like Bill's second child. It's like he's lost both of his children. You were the last one to see Emmett. You owe it to him. You owe it to ME! I was there for you, remember. I did something for you, no one else would EVER do." He's yelling now.

I put him on speaker phone, so I don't have to hear him yell so loudly next to my ear. I see I have a notification from my bank—I click on it and tune out my dad, who is still yelling about something. I have heard it all before.

A transfer from Layla has gone through to my account. We agreed on two payments, one now at the beginning and one after three months. At that time, she will evaluate if she wants to continue my services; that is, if I haven't found her someone by then. Will I be able to find someone for her in just three months?

"Dad," I cut off his rant. "I am not going to come home anytime soon." No matter what he says, no matter how loud he gets, I never cave, not when it comes to going back to Utah—even for a short visit.

"I just don't understand, Madi." He has lowered his tone, but is still stern and angry. I do feel slightly bad. I know my dad did the best he knew how, raising me alone after Mom died, but I also don't feel bad; I cannot go back there, no matter what.

"You don't have to Dad. I have to go. I'll send some money." I hang up the phone before he can say anything else. He will call in a few weeks, repeating this exact conversation. This is the only consistent thing I can count on him for.

I take a few breaths before focusing on Layla and finding her a date. I glance at my notes, refreshing my memory of her preferences:

Age range: 27-35
Height range: 5'5"+
Physical aspects: dark hair, athletic

She focused more on personality than looks when we were discussing the type of man she wants in her life.

Personality: must love dogs, care about health and being healthy, outgoing, love outdoors, love trying new restaurants, more spiritual than religious, wants a family, ready for a meaningful relationship

I keep everything in mind while I swipe through profiles. Left is a no and right is a yes. So far, I have swiped most of them to the left; only about four or five of them got a right swipe. It seems like every time I put my phone down, Layla's profile gains another 15 likes. I finally made it to the last five for today.

Randy, 30, Houston
Bio:

The bio is blank. There is no more information about him on the profile, except for four photos: one selfie, one full-body, one covering his face, and one close up of his face. Swipe left.

Tony, 31, Engineer, Houston
Bio: Multi-business owner from Dallas looking for someone that isn't afraid to be adventurous and fun. Love traveling, exploring new cities and cultures any time I get a chance!
Looking for long-term relationship
6'
Grad school degree
No kids, but wants kids
From Dallas, Texas
Interests: Reading, Traveling, Dogs, Restaurants, Running
Prompt 1: If I could live anywhere in the world for one year, I would live...in France.
Prompt 2: My favorite quote is... "Life teaches, love reveals."
Prompt 3: The 3 words that best describe me are...honest, creative, loving.

"Okay, okay Tony. I see you with this complete profile." I say aloud—I've been talking to myself a lot lately—I really should stop or at least get a cat.

Tony's first picture is a head shot of him clearly in business casual clothes. He is clean shaven, his dark brown hair styled short, his green eyes pierce through the camera. The next photo is a full-body photo of him in casual, but nice clothes, standing with the Houston night skyline behind him. The third and final photo is of Tony in workout clothes standing outside, in this photo you can see he is fit. I swipe right.

Erik, 30, Inspector, Houston
*Bio: A few words...impossible! Emojis the more the merrier or something like that *shrug emoji**
Looking for something casual

I don't finish looking at the profile—swipe left.

TJ, 29, Manager, Houston
Bio: Recently moved to Houston, show me around!
Looking for something long-term
5'11"
College degree
No kids, but wants kids
From Kansas City, Missouri
Interests: Gym, Running, Basketball, Watching TV &

Movies, Listening to Music
Prompt 1: The 3 words that best describe me are...strong,
ambitious, kind

TJ's first photo is of him sitting at a table, wearing a hat, smiling—he has a warm smile. I keep scrolling through the other photos. He has a gym photo that shows his full-body; thankfully, it's not a cringey flex gym photo. I keep going; the next photo is with a friend; his friend is cute, focus Madison. His final photo is of him leaning up against a mural wall downtown. I swipe right on TJ. I can picture him taking Layla on a nice date.

Leonard, 27, Talent Manager, Houston
Bio: I am a nature love—I love spending time outdoors and
I'm also looking for a new hiking trail to explore.
Looking for something long-terms
6'1"
College degree
From Dallas, Texas
Interests: Hiking, Anime, Music, Reading

Leonard has five photos. They range from full-body to just his face to a few selfies. He has dark features and is very handsome. His jaw is defined and I think I can see abs through his shirt in one of the photos. While Layla didn't focus on physical aspect, it's all I have to go on in this application. Leonard would look good next to Layla—swipe right—we will see if his personality fits too.

I have finally made it through all of the likes Layla has so far; I see private messages have come through already, which means the men have seen she liked their profiles as well. Instead of starting to respond, I close the application and throw my phone on the bed. The exhaustion hits me as I lay back, staring up at the ceiling, losing my thoughts in the fan.

Detective Oliver

"You look like shit." Liam hands me a cup of coffee.

I look at him and the cup, my nose wrinkling without permission—I know he's only filled up a cup with the stale coffee from the break room, but they say it's the thought that counts.

"You couldn't get us some good coffee? Oh and thank you for the compliment."

"You know they don't pay me enough for anything better than Starbies for anyone but myself."

"Starbies?" I roll my eyes. Liam is younger than I am, but he's not that young—still he always comes in with a new acronym or slang that the young crowd is saying, making me feel much older than I am. He just smiles and shrugs.

I start walking to my office and he follows.

"What's that?" I finally notice he has a folder in his hands.

"I was going to wait until you put your stuff down. They identified the body last night."

I rip the folder out of his hands, almost spilling the coffee on Aida, a fellow detective whose desk we were passing.

"Liam! What have I told you about burying the lead!" I don't open the folder until I have made it into my office and set down all of my things. It's heavier than I expected.

"He's got a lengthy past." Liam says reading my mind.

Tomas Elian Mark, 32, Houston, Texas

I lift my eyebrow at Liam. He rolls his eyes and motions for me to continue.

The report lists his current home address, previous addresses, phone numbers, closest known relatives, and other general information. There is a picture—his driver's license picture. Tomas looks like he was a bigger guy than the one they pulled from the bayou. According to the license, he has brown eyes, brown hair, and five foot, eight. I take a deep breath before continuing.

The first offense against him—assault. I scan the report, glazing over the details. A woman filed it against him for punching her in the face at a club. The second report against him—theft of property. The third report—sexual assault. Fourth charge—sexual assault. I flip through the rest of the papers; assault, theft, battery, robbery—the reports just keep going and going. How was this man not in jail?

"Real piece of crap, huh?!" Liam says. "I read through each of them. He should have been in jail years ago."

"Yea, he should have been. But all these reports were filed by women." It shouldn't mean anything, but it does.

"Mmm." I can't tell if Liam agrees or doesn't; not that he has to.

"Have we contacted the family?"

"I was going to call his parents this morning."

"PLEASE, MR., MRS. MARK, have a seat." Liam has led the Marks to an office at the station that looks a little less like an interrogation room—there's not many.

"It's not Mrs. Mark anymore. Just call me Rose." Tomas's mom says as she sits.

"What is this about?" Tomas Mark, not senior—we were informed, Rose chose a different middle name for their son, so he couldn't officially call himself Senior or his son Junior.

Liam and I sit across from the couple.

"When is the last time either of you saw your son?" I let Liam take the lead this time.

"Oh, for fucks sakes. What has he done now?" Rose rolls her eyes.

"He hasn't done anything, not exactly. When is the last time you saw him?"

"It's been about six or more months. Whatever trouble he has gotten himself into, I don't want any part of it." Rose starts to stand, I assume she is trying to leave already.

"He's dead, ma'am." I instantly regret the blunt words as they escape my mouth. Rose crumbles back into the seat.

"What?" Tomas questions.

"I'm sorry to inform you both. Tomas Elian Mark was found in the Buffalo Bayou deceased. We were able to identify his body through DNA."

"Are you sure it's him?" Tomas asked.

"Positive. We are so sorry for your loss."

"Can we see him?" Rose asks.

"That's not the best idea. He was in the water for a long time. I don't think you want to remember him like that."

"What happened?" Rose starts crying.

"We are trying to figure that out."

"You don't think we had anything to do with it?!" Tomas bursts.

"Right now we are trying to gather as much information as possible to piece together exactly what happened to Tomas."

"I haven't seen him in almost a year." Tomas spits as he speaks.

Honestly, we were surprised Tomas was coming in to talk with us today—based on his record he has either spent the last six years in prison or in Louisiana. We were unsure of where he was located now, but when Liam called, he said he would bring Rose in with him.

"What was your relationship with Tomas like?" Again, I regretted the question; this was not the line of questioning Liam and I discussed before we walked in here.

"Strained. I'll admit. Mostly my fault. I was in and out of jail his whole life." Tomas sighs. "Drugs are killer man." I'm surprised by his honesty. I glance at Rose.

"I swear I'm clean now," he pleads; I'm not sure if to me, or to Rose.

"Our relationship was strained too. Mine and my son's, well mine and my husband's too. Well I guess we can't call him my husband anymore." Tears fill her eyes, again. "Tomas, struggled his whole life. In school, with people, with girls. He was accused of a lot of things. I tired not to believe them, but I don't know. He was just so troubled."

"Do you know if he has any close friends that we can contact?" Liam asks.

"I don't. Like I said, it's been months. I think he had lost his job when he came around asking for money the last time. I gave him some and hadn't seen him since." Rose sounds sincere.

"Do you know if Tomas was dating anyone?"

"I mean he always had a girl. Or someone around him. But I never knew any of them," she says.

"Is there anyone else that you can think of that could be helpful here?" I ask.

They both shake their head. They really don't know anything about their son's life. Looks like, we are on our own to try to figure out what happened to Tomas.

"Do you think he would harm himself?" Liam asks.

"I don't even know. I don't know my son the way I should." Tomas looks down suddenly, hands flexing, breath hitching—like something inside him just snapped into place, too late to fix.

They insisted on seeing his body against more encouragement not to. Aida walks them to Ashley's office—I would rather not see their reaction to their son in morgue.

"Welcome to the Color Factory!" A thin, brown eyed high school student greeted the group as we walked from the lobby into the first colorful room. "First, you can grab a treat to your left, take a photo off to your right, and then line up at the next door where I will go over the rules."

I look up at James—it was his idea to come here today. His students had told him it was a fun, immersive, colorful experience he needed to share with his wife. Well, they didn't say all that. Actually they told him, he should go but do it high and leave his cop wife at home. I laughed and agreed with them. James didn't find it funny.

We each grab a different color fortune cookie and take a silly picture. The employee hands us a card to use throughout for pictures that we will be able to purchase at the end of the experience. I put on a smile, but this isn't exactly the type of place I want to spend my Saturday at. I drown out the "rules" of the place—you'd think, as a cop I would be more of a rule follower, and generally I am, but not in a place like this. I didn't always follow the laws growing up, especially junior year of high school. James on the other hand, always followed all rules and laws. He prides himself on the fact that he's never done a drug his whole life.

The hallway winds with the black and white stripes painted floor to ceiling. Giant balls bouncing, being thrown around. James tosses a purple one my way. I take it to the air being forced through the floor in certain areas. The ball shoots to the ceiling.

"See, science, cool." James laughs at himself. I laugh at him, too.

We keep making our way to the next room.

"Nope!" I say too loudly as soon as we step into the room filled with tiny bits of colorful paper. A kid runs by throwing a big handful of confetti, I jump back so far, I hit my back against the wall.

James laughs, but comes to me. "Are you okay?"

"I'm fine. But we need to get out of here, now!" I tip toe the best I can, so no tiny piece of paper gets stuck to my shoes.

We make it to a room that was not only completely black but also completely dark besides some black lighting. I was confused by the room at first.

"Oh! It's like a lite brite!" I exclaim.

"A what?"

"What do you mean, what? Did you not have one of these as a child?" I pick up a colored tube and stick it in a hole in the wall, the tube lights up yellow.

James just watches as I put more tubes in holes, creating a bright yellow and purple flower on the wall. He pulls me close to him, leaning down to kiss my forehead.

We keep making our way through the place, room after room.

"You want to jump in the ball pit?" I mock James.

He shakes his head. "Now, that's where I draw the line."

On the other side of the ball pit area, we were handed black ice cream cones—interesting choice for ice cream at a colorful place. I pulled out my phone as we enjoy our ice cream. I shake it off before I think too much about it.

"What's wrong?" James notices the shift in my face immediately.

I shake my head. "I don't know. I have so many missed calls from Liam."

"Take it."

"Are you sure? I don't want to ruin our day."

"Yes," he nods. "Go do what you need to do."

I step outside and call Liam back without listening to any of the five voice mails he left me. It's got to be important; he knows not to disrupt my weekends off.

"What's up, Liam?" I ask hastily, without a hello.

"We've got another body."

"What? More words Liam."

"They just pulled another body from the bayou."

"Okay? I'm not sure why this was urgent enough to call me on a Saturday."

"I thought you might want to know. It might be connected to our first one."

"Let's not jump to conclusions, Liam. Make sure you do the usual and get the body to Ashley's lab."

"I don't know, Detective." He takes an audible breath. "Two male bodies pulled from the Buffalo Bayou. Seems like there may be a connection."

"There may be a connection, Liam. But at this point we just cannot make that conclusion. Let's see what evidence you can find at the scene and what Ashley and her team can figure out first."

"Okay."

"We'll figure this out, Liam. Whether they are connected or not."

"Everything okay?" James asks as he walks out of the place, handing me a copy of the photo we took at the beginning of the trip.

I laugh. "What is this?"

"A photo," he mocks.

"Did you pay for this?"

He nods and I shake my head taking the image from his hands—I'll admit it was actually a good photo of us.

"Everything okay with work?"

"I don't know, honestly. Another body was found in the bayou this morning."

"A second one?"

I nod. "Yea. Liam thinks they are connected."

"What do you think?"

"I don't know. I need to see the body and the evidence. You know I don't jump to conclusions."

He kisses me. "I know. You follow the evidence. Any breaks in the first case?"

"No, not beyond actually finding out who he was. We were supposed to search is apartment yesterday, but the judge didn't sign the search warrant until late in the day."

He sighs, in solidarity frustration for me. "Do you want to go in?"

I sigh. He knows I want to, but we also had this whole day planned out, just for us. I don't want to give up this time with James either.

"I can see it in your face. You want to go in."

I wrinkle my nose at him. "You know I do. But also, I really don't. I want to spend this time here with you."

"Well, we are done here." Here, meaning the The Color Factory, but I know James has more planned for the day.

"I know. But, I'd love to continue the day with you." I pull him close, as we walk to the car.

"Are you sure?" He opens the car door for me.

"Absolutely positive."

Madison

MESSAGE FROM SPENCER:

> What a stunning woman. All I'd ever want to do is keep a smile on your face and give you this passionate bedroom loving all night. San Diego or Miami? Snuggler or it's hot? Planner or go with the flow? Hiking or beach?

What is this message?! I click on his name, which takes me to his profile—I hadn't seen this one before, so I didn't swipe right before he messaged—I didn't even know that was possible. Spencer is a 5'9", blonde, brown-eyed, beautiful man. He has so much potential. However, that message—big turn off! I delete the message and move on to the next.

Message from Tony:

> Good morning, Layla! Your dog is adorable, I'd love to take you and him out for a walk with my puppy some-time.

Oh okay, Tony, starting off strong with acknowledging the most important thing in Layla's life right off the bat. Also, suggesting an activity is a great first date. I message him back to continue the conversation.

> Good morning, Tony! Thank you, I'd love to take the pups on a walk some-time. What kind of dog do you have?

Message from Leonard:

> Hi! How are you?

Leonard, a little boring, but I'll accept it. My general rule, I just made up, is going to reply to the messages as long as they don't open with anything inappropriate (e.g., Spencer's message).

Message to Leonard:

> Hi! I'm great! How are you?

Message from Deven:

> Hello Beautiful! How are you?

> Hello! I'm great! How are you?

I continue with the same message to two more men who sent the same exact 'Hi, how are you?' messages.

Message from Chad:

> Thank you for gracing me with your present. My name is Chad. I like to know you better. You don't be disappointed.

I think I got a migraine reading that message. I can never tell, when reading messages like that if it's a catfish or just a man that can't type out a coherent message. Either way, it doesn't actually matter; it's an automatic delete. All said and done, I have five conversations going for Layla so far. She has more matches I need to go through.

I will continue these conversations for Layla and continue swiping left and right until one of them works out for her. I won't stop, nor will I move onto helping any other woman until I find Layla someone to date.

"How is your actual first ghost dating client going?" Ellie asks on our weekly video call.

"It's going well!" I grab my tablet. "I think. Let me read you some of their messages." I switch our call to my tablet and open the dating application on my phone. I read the messages from Tony, including the latest one I hadn't seen yet.

> I have a lab mix. Would Tuesday at 6p at Hermann Park work for you to walk the dogs and get to know each other?

"Well, he got straight to the point," Ellie says.

"Yes, I actually like that, I hate when men just want to message back and forth for weeks on end. Like what's the point of that?"

Ellie agrees. "So is Layla going to meet up with him in a few days?"

"I have to get his actual number, so I can research him a little. I don't want to send her on a date with a serial killer." I laugh, but it's a real threat.

Ellie nods along as I continue. "With his number I will be able to gather a lot more information and make sure he's not married and all that. I really hate that I have to do all this just for a woman to go on a date."

"I know, men are shit." Ellie laughs, knowing she married an actual good one.

"So are women," I counter.

"Touche," she says. "Did you do a background check on Nick?"

"I never told you the amount of digging I did on Nick."

After I told Ellie about Nick, I found all of his social media accounts, his mother's accounts, his high school transcript, and his first girlfriend's name. I considered reaching out to one of them to find out more, but figure that would be a little too stalker-ish.

"You never told me! But you were right about him. You're always right," she rolls her eyes. I just smile and shrug her off. Looking back at the messages from Tony, I ponder what to respond.

"Where's Kevin?" Ellie breaks the silence.

I awkwardly cough, almost choking on my saliva. "Oh, he's at work tonight."

"That man works too much! How do y'all have time for a relationship? When will I ever get to meet him?"

I dart my eyes away from the tablet and stare at the wall while answering her question. "I know. It can be challenging, but you know I like my alone time anyway." Ellie and

I are vastly different in that way—she loves being around people and I'd rather be alone.

"Yea, but you need time together too. And I need to meet him!" her voice is slightly raised. "I mean, how are you going to get engaged to a man your best friend hasn't even met!"

Still not looking at her, I say, "I know, I know. With school and work, he's just so busy."

We have the same conversation every two or three weeks. Ellie just sighs and drops the subject. She starts talking about a special accounting project she was put on at work—I tune her out, not understanding most of what she is saying. We finally say our goodbyes and will talk next week.

MY CELL PHONE ILLUMINATES in my hand—*how did the screen brightness get turned up so much?* I stay focused on my tasks, navigating to the dating app, to message Tony.

> I'd love to take the dogs for a walk Tuesday. Can I get your phone number?

It's forward, so I hope he doesn't get scared. But maybe, if he gets scared from something like that, he isn't the right man for Layla.

Message to Leonard:

> I am a nurse at a hospital in the med center. What is it that you do?

> They gave me a fancy title of talent manager - i.e. I'm a recruiter. Out of these, which one would you say is your favorite? Coffee, walking, ice cream.

Leonard's message came through as soon as I had messaged him. Should I wait a little while before replaying? They say there's a fine line between interest and desperation. However, he clearly has been on his phone and in the application at the same time to respond so quickly. Let's not play silly little games.

> Ice cream, definitely ice cream. Well, I love them all, but you said I could only pick one.

I close the application and toss my phone in my gym back—now, I'm going to be late for spin class.

Beep. Beep. Beep.

"Hey guys! This is a good question, Jessica asks about my success rate. I want to be as transparent with you all as possible. My first match-making experience was in college, and it was actually in person. I set my best friend up with her now husband. The next two clients were through apps. In those cases, I took my friend's phones, did initial swiping, and initial messages for them. The men I matched them with and started conversations with ended up being amazing. One of the couples is still together to this day. The other couple didn't work out for various reasons. This is my first endeavor doing this for strangers. I do have my first client from one of you wonderful followers. However, with respect to her privacy, I will give updates but limited. Keep your questions, comments, and DMs coming! I will get to them as quickly as I can." *#ghostdating*

I make sure to smile before stopping the recording. I thought I'd blow a kiss at the end of all my videos, however, I don't always remember and I don't like to rerecord just for that. The initial video I posted has gotten thousands more views, likes, and comments. I also have ton of direct messages that I am trying to work through. I decided I only want to work with one client right now, until I get the process down and then I can add more clients.

ARMED WITH TONY'S PHONE number, I find his full legal name, his address, and all of his social media accounts. I cannot find any evidence of any kids, any marriages, or any criminal records. It appears his profile is truthful and so far has kept everything above board. His social media accounts are mostly private, the few posts or photos I can see, are all a few years back—which I understand; most of my social media accounts are the same. I text Layla.

> Hey! I am sending you screenshots of a profile and messages. Tony—seems like a great guy. He wants to meet Tuesday to walk the dogs together. I think that's a super cute idea. I have ran my initial background check and everything checks out. He isn't married and doesn't have any kids. Let me know what you think of his profile.

> Girl! Yes. He is exactly my type and super cute! I am free Tuesday, surprisingly, so I could meet him.

> I thought so! Awesome! I am so excited for you. I am going to text him now from the virtual phone number we discussed. You should be able to see the messages and take over on your side.

Since Layla is onboard with Tony, I switch over to text him.

> *Hey, it's Layla! I'd love to take our dogs for a walk Tuesday. Is that still good for you?*

Tony responds quickly confirming he is still available Tuesday at 6pm and for them to meet at Hermann Park. I let Layla respond as herself, however, as long as they use this text messaging application, I can see their messages.

Maybe I should be at the park, just in case Layla needs someone there while meeting a stranger—*would that be weird?* I switch back to the dating application to find new messages for Layla.

Message from Austin:

> Hey! How are you?

> Hey! I am great! How are you?

Message from David:

hey

hey

Message from Leonard:

Ice cream, good choice. Let's figure out a time next week we are both free and I can take you to the best ice cream in town.

Message from CJ:

get this big, long, shlong waiting on your pretty face

Oh my god! No wonder so many women hate dating sites so much. I click on CJ's profile to remind myself why I swiped right in the first place, not that it matters really. He looks like such an innocent, "normal" 28-year-old. His profile even says he is looking for something long-term. I guess that was a lie to get more matches. I unmatch and delete the message.

I click on Leonard's profile before replying to his message. That's right, he was the other man I swiped right on that I really like for Layla; so I message him back.

> Would love to get ice cream next week. Can I get your number and I'll text to coordinate?

I don't even know why I message David back at all—but I'll match his energy and see what his next move is. Honestly, you never know with how interactions on these kinds of applications can turn into. However, I do think if someone can't even capitalize a word, they are lazy and it won't lead to a meaningful conversation.

Text to Layla:

> I'm so happy you are going to meet with Tony. I am sending you another profile and screenshots of messages. I like this guy Leonard for you too.

Layla doesn't respond right away, and neither to any of the men on the dating site. I close it all out and pull up the last video I posted. It has thousands of views, which is insane—I never would have thought so many people would be interested in anything I was doing. And I don't really know how I feel about it yet.

"WHAT HAS YOU SO distracted today?" Robbie asks, standing over my cubicle, as he does. I didn't even see him there and I'm not sure how long he has been there staring at me.

"Who says I'm distracted? I am just busy." I try to play it off, but all I can think about it Layla's date with Tony tonight. She has strict instructions to call me right after the date. She has also agreed to get ice cream with Leonard on Friday. I am so excited and giddy for her but also so nervous—I feel like a parent sending their child off to war or something.

"That email you sent me made no sense." I look up and he is rolling his eyes.

"It made perfect sense!" I protest, while pulling the email up on my computer. I read through the message.

"Okay," I give up. "Maybe I am a little distracted." Robbie smirks as if he has won something.

"Everything okay?" Lauri chimes in. "It's not Kevin, is it? What did he do?"

I laugh and look away from them. "No, actually, I've been looking at wedding venues. It's overwhelming," I lie.

"Ooooh!" Robbie claps. "I love that. Let me help! Also, I am so proud. You are finally making progress on wedding planning. About damn time. Did you pick a date?"

Still avoiding eye contact, I shake my head. "Not yet. I was thinking about seeing about venues and their availability, then going from there."

"That's not how it works, Madi."

"Why not? I don't really care when." I finally look at Robbie, he reads the exhaustion in my face—I am over this conversation.

He rolls his eyes, again. "Madi, you need so much help. I don't understand how you are able to help others so much, but can't help yourself."

Heat rises in my cheeks.

Before I say anything I might regret, Robbie says, "Don't worry, babe! I'll take care of you." He blows a kiss as he starts sauntering off.

I take deep breaths, blowing the air out through my teeth. If Lauri notices, she doesn't say anything. Twenty minutes later, I have a spreadsheet in my inbox labeled 'Wedding Planning!!!!' I don't even open it, I just delete it—I won't be needing a wedding planning document. Also, I need different friends, too many spreadsheets keep popping into my inbox.

Detective Oliver

"Have you seen this?" James leans over in bed, showing me his phone.

"What is it?" I ask taking his phone from him, starting the video he had paused.

"A male body was found in the Buffalo Bayou this morning. This is the second body..." I cut the video. The text over video says "Is a woman leading men into the water to their demise in the bayou?!"

"Shit." I say, handing back his phone, and jumping out of bed.

"Do you have any leads on the cases?"

I shake my head, to answer his question and at the media sensationalizing this case. "We have nothing so far," I sigh.

"Do you think a woman murdered these men? Was the second body even a man?" he asks.

"No clue. Liam texted more about the second body, but didn't really give a lot of details. I've got to get to work."

I HEAD STRAIGHT FOR the medical examiner's office before even setting foot in my office. Liam texted a few times over the weekend, still convinced these two cases are connected—I want to see the body first and get Ashley's professional opinion.

"Good morning, Grace." Ashley greets me with a big, white smile.

"Good morning, Ashley." I try to give her a smile back, but my stomach churned as soon as I walked into the office.

Ashley puts on blue, latex gloves. "I hope you aren't here about this body." She points to the water-logged man—it's definitely another man—on her examination table.

"Yup. That would be exactly why I am here."

"I just got in this morning. I wasn't working this weekend and my crew had some other bodies to work on when this one was found. It's going to be a while before I can tell you anything."

"I understand. I didn't think you'd have a full report worked up yet, although I know if anyone would, you would." I give her a wink.

"Oh, stop. Giving me compliments isn't going to make me work faster." She pulls the plastic sheet off the man's body. At least this body seems to be intact.

"I'm not trying to rush you, I swear. Liam just thinks these two pulled from the bayou are connected. And apparently so does the media," I roll my eyes. "I don't want to jump to any conclusions."

"Yea, I saw a few videos about that. I'll let you know of any similarities for sure. I do know, they took his DNA and fingerprints already. So you might be able to identify this one a lot quicker."

"Thanks, Ashley." I choke down my words on the verge of throwing up.

"Are you okay, Grace?"

I shake my head, but pull my hand up to my mouth, as if that will stop anything that might want to make it's way up.

"This is the second time you've gotten sick in my lab." She states, matter-of-factly. I really didn't think she noticed the first time.

I nod. "It's like the millionth time I've gotten sick in the last few weeks. It's so weird."

"Grace," she pauses. "Are you pregnant?"

I stop breathing. "What? No. That's impossible."

Ashley stares at me; a mix between concern and curiosity across her face. No, I can't be pregnant—the doctor said that was near impossible.

"Knock, knock." I look up, Liam stands, brows pinched together, like he's silently asking why I'm just standing here at my desk. He shakes away the question, stepping inside.

"Can whatever you came in here for wait?" My words land too sharp. He nods and backs out of my office.

I slip out of my office, moving fast—too fast for a normal walk, too slow to be a run—hoping it reads as casual. My breathing too quick, my pulse thunders in my ears, head down, hoping no one stops me.

"Ohmygod! Is this thing broken?!" I yell, as I shake the pregnancy test I peed on only thirty seconds ago. The box said to wait 3 minutes, but I'm impatient. I'm also in the station bathroom—I don't want anyone walking in seeing me with this thing.

I stare at myself in the mirror. They, many doctors, said I most likely would not be able to get pregnant. Not that they could find anything wrong. Both James and I got all the tests offered; every single one came back inconclusive.

I guess they never said it could *never* happen, but that it probably wouldn't. I hadn't even considered it a possibility until Ashley mentioned it this morning.

I can't believe I missed a period and didn't catch it; of course, I track it on two separate applications and in my calendar. It had to have happened before this case, so I can't even blame stress and work.

I look down at the white and blue stick in my hand. PREGNANT

I blink. The word is still there. I almost sink to the floor, but hold myself up gripping the counter. My breath catches in my throat, half-laugh, half-sob, like my body can't decide what to feel first. I press my free hand to my stomach, grounding myself as the room tilts. After years of probably not, it's happening. It's actually happening.

"Everything okay?" Liam asks when we pull up to Tomas's apartment.

"Yup." The pregnancy shock has worn off and excitement has taken it's place. I spent the rest of the morning thinking of different ways I can tell James. As excited as I am, I want him to be the first person I tell.

"Sorry about earlier," I offer an apology.

"No worries."

"Where are we?" I ask.

"Tomas's place."

"I know," I roll my eyes.

I wasn't paying attention to what neighborhood we drove to. It doesn't look like one of the best ones for sure. Liam didn't answer my question, he just got out of the car. We had two other cop cars park behind us.

"Number 312, we have arrived." Liam exclaims after we walk up to the third floor of the small building.

He knocks and I hope no one is there—the landlord stated Tomas lived alone, or at least only his name was on the lease. No one answers the door and Liam opens it. Officer Newsome, a rookie, enters first announcing that we are the police. She sweeps the apartment to ensure no one is inside before the rest of us enter. As expected, there is no one in the place. Still a little apprehensive, we all gather in the small apartment.

Calling this an apartment is generous. It's barely a box with four walls. Even the walls look flimsy. Sitting on a counter, what I assume to be the kitchen, is a burned up microwave. I look at Liam, disgusted.

"His place is just as bad as his rap sheet, huh?" Liam jokes.

"What would you like me to do, Detective?" Officer Newsome asks.

"Can you bag and tag his computer first? Looking around," I actively sweep my eyes corner to corner. "It doesn't seem like there is a lot here."

"Grace, come see what's in the closet."

I follow Liam's voice to the closet. Three shirts are haphazardly hung, some shoe boxes thrown across the floor, and four guns shoved in a corner. Liam didn't call me over to look at the shoe boxes. I sigh.

"Let's get those out of here." I tell him.

While they are bagging those few items, I start opening cabinets in the kitchen—there's only two doors and one drawer.

"Ugh!"

"What is it?" Liam asks.

"Pills."

"Not surprising, huh?" He comes around peering into the drawer. "What are these?"

"Looks like Adderall." I sigh. "We'll have the lab test it, of course."

"I'll get them bagged for you," Officer Newsome says.

"Thank you."

"You think he was taking those himself? Or selling?" Liam asks.

I shrug—doesn't really matter now. "It would be enough to charge him for intent to distribute. But I've seen people with more who weren't trying to sell."

"Doesn't matter now, I suppose," he says reading my mind. "Who was this man?"

I shoulders go up and down, again. It's not our job to figure out who he was, it's our job to figure out what happened to him.

Madison

"Tell me everything!" I say instead of hello, answering Layla's call on the first ring. I was just staring at my phone all evening—making sure it was plugged in, so it doesn't die before we got to talk.

Layla is glowing and blushing at the same time. She takes a deep breath.

"It was amazing. We met at the park. Our dogs actually got along. We walked and talked for almost two hours!"

"So...the conversation was good?"

She nods her head. "It was so good. Flowed so naturally, there was no lulls in the conversation at all. Easy."

"Did y'all have chemistry too?"

"So much chemistry! I was so surprised. He looked just like his photos, he's handsome. I am extremely attracted to him. I feel so crazy because I feel so giddy." She finally breathes. "I don't want to get too excited though." She sighs, saying so much with just a breath out.

"It's okay to get excited and have these feelings! Even if it was a first date. Get hopeful. The problem with that arises when we play out scenarios in our head of future things with people. That's when we fall in love with the fantasy and not the real person."

"Yea, you're right," Layla agrees.

"And you have another date in a few days. It's good to keep your options open."

"Yes, I'm kind of hesitant to go on the date with Leonard now. It already feels weird with how things went with..." she trails off, but smiles at the phone. "Tony just texted."

"You're blushing!" I gush. "What did he say?"

"Oh, just that he really enjoyed our walk and wants to make plans to see each other soon. He's asking about weekend plans." I know she isn't telling me the full message, which is fine because it's personal.

"See what I mean. I got butterflies seeing his name pop up already. I might feel guilty going out with another man."

"Girl, no. Not at this point. Again, I think it's for the best to see what else is out there. If you still feel this way about Tony after the date with Leonard, then you can just see him. I don't advice this approach, but I don't want to make you uncomfortable or do anything you don't want to do."

"I know, you're right, again."

"Also, there's a few men that I matched you with that had started conversations, but have since fell off. Do you want me to just let those go at this point? And any new matches or conversations?"

"I think so. I don't think I can do more than two first dates with different men, at this point."

"Okay, okay. I am going to go through the app now. We will put it on pause for now."

She nods. "And we can always pick it up later, if necessary?" I can see her hesitation—this is why I want to do this for women; dating is so time consuming and exhausting.

"Yes, of course."

We say our goodbyes and she promises she will call again after her ice cream date with Leonard.

Message from Clare:

Hi! I have typed and deleted this message so many times. I feel like I sound so desperate. But I so need your help! OH. My name is Clare and I am new to Houston from Seattle. I have had such a terrible time dating here. I am not very confident on the apps. I've been catfished, lied to, send dick pics. But I really want to find my person. I want to settle down with that person, build a future together. I want to be in a happy, healthy relationship. Do you think you could help me? It's okay if you never respond to this message.

Good morning, Clare! I feel you so much in your message. Dating in a new city can be so tough, I did it years ago myself. I hate you have had a bunch of negative experiences here too. I would love to help you and I have just wrapped up with my first client. Please fill out the form linked in my bio and we will have a video call to get started! Much love!!

I sign the message with a blue heart emoji. Since Layla has narrowed down to two men already and won't require dating application attention, I think it's time to take on another client—Ellie would be so proud. Clare's message wasn't the next in line on my direct messages, but I really felt she needed help the most.

Text from Layla:

Ice cream with Leonard was good.
Let's talk later?

I am so glad ice cream went well. Can't wait for the details. Talk tonight!

"BREATH IN, OUT. TAKE child's pose here if needed." The yoga instructor prompted as she walked around assisting with some complicated body contortion she told everyone to try. I've been in child's pose for the last 10 minutes. My focus and attention is not here in this class; I step out to take a call.

"Hi, love!" Layla is sitting in front of an overflowing bookshelf.

"Hi, Madison!" Her face the color of a just ripened strawberry.

"What are you blushing about?" I call her out, even though I would have hated someone doing that to me.

She puts her head down, embarrassed. "Oh, I just got off a call with Tony." She looks up smiling and it's contagious. "I know it's so soon, but I'm so...I don't even know."

Watching her beam reminds me, again, why I wanted to do this for women in the first place. I want to see women having a positive, meaningful dating experience. This is what dating should be like—not swiping left and right on strangers; not the horror stories I've heard about.

"Let's back up a minute." I start walking out of the yoga studio. "Tell me about the ice cream date with Leonard."

She takes a deep breath. "Okay, we had a great time! Like I really connected with him too. He was very attentive to the conversation, it flowed well, and we have a lot in common."

"Oh, I just knew you guys would hit it off."

"But," she pauses.

I breathe out. "But?"

"I just feel more of a connection with Tony at this point. Is it bad to just focus on that right now?"

"I think you need to do what you are most comfortable with for sure. Just make sure you reach out to Leonard and tell him you guys are not moving forward."

Her head drops, again. "Yea, I mentioned I was dating other people. He was really cool about it and he's dating others as well."

"So back to Tony, then. Tell me, do you have plans to see each other again?"

Layla's face lights back up. "Yes, we have dinner plans tonight. At a nice place downtown."

"You are so happy, I love this for you!"

"I can't believe this happened so fast! Thank you so much! I really don't know how to thank you."

I am happy Layla seems happy with Tony so far, but I suddenly get a twinge in my gut, a slow churn that feels like a warning. *Is this happening too fast? Does she need to slow down and take a step back?* I get a momma bear sense of protection that I can't shake. However, she is an adult and she can make her own decisions.

"I know. Please still keep your eye out for any red flags that might pop up. And please, please keep me updated on how things keep progressing."

She agrees and we hang up. The terrible feeling in my gut doesn't immediately dissipate.

I dial Clare's number and she answers on the first ring. We had scheduled this video call through messages, so I guess she was ready and waiting by her phone—as I would have been.

"Hi!" Clare is glowing and excited.

"Hi!" I fumble setting up my phone, so I don't have to hold it while talking to her—I should have done it before I called, but alas.

"So, sorry." I take a deep breath. "How are you, Clare?" I finally ask.

"I'm great! You?"

"I am good. Sorry, just getting setup here. I swear I am normally more organized. Today has just been a bit hectic."

"Oh I understand, no worries. I was surprised you even answered my message in the first place."

I finally have my phone setup and notebook and pen ready to go. I laugh.

"Yea, I was honestly surprised at all the messages I got. I didn't think anyone would even see that video, let alone so many women reaching out, needing, and wanting help."

"Of course. Dating right now is so awful!" I nod in agreement.

"I know."

I explain the ghost dating process and pricing structure. Clare agrees to the same plan that Layla did. We discuss her dating history, what she is looking for in terms of someone to date, what she wants in a relationship, and everything in between. Before I know it, we have been talking for two and a half hours, and I have eight pages of notes.

"I saw your last video about your success. But since you've started this, you have had one other client?"

I close my notebook. "Yes, you would be my second client from my video, officially. The first message I received from my initial video because my first client."

"And you have already found her person?!" The shock radiates through the phone.

"In a sense. With keeping her privacy, the first man I set her up with. She had a real connection with him and wants to see where that goes."

"Oh wow! You got it on the first try?! I mean I was confident in your abilities, but that's fast and nuts!"

"We shall see how it progresses," I shrug. My gut twists again.

"I will say, learning that gives me some hope. Although you know, I will try anything at this point." She sighs.

"I know, I know. I am going to create your profile tonight and start this for you! I am excited and hopeful."

Clare, 26, Pilates Studio Owner, Houston
Bio: Passionate about helping others feel their best, whether it's through a plank or meaningful conversations. I'm looking for someone who values growth, laughter, and a healthy lifestyle. Let's build something strong together, inside and out.
Looking for long-term relationship
5'1"
College degree
No kids, but wants kids
From Seattle, Washington
Interests: Pilates, Walking, Reading, Meditation, Restaurants
Prompt 1: My healthy obsession is...collagen in my morning brew!
Prompt 2: Instead of drinks...let's try something new.

Just like Layla, Clare's profile gets a ton of attention—there are about 90 men who have initially liked her profile in only eight hours. I start going through them, of course swiping left on most of them.

Brandon, 33, Greeter, Houston
Bio: Looking for my partner in crime. Interesting in dating
1 woman.
Looking for something casual
5'8"
From Maryland

I'm sorry, what Brandon? You want to date only one person but also want that to be casual? How does that even make sense? I don't even scroll to see his pictures or any more information. Swipe left.

Kerry, 21, Police Officer, Woodlands
Bio: Highly motivated individual with big dreams. Looking
for someone to grow and spend life with.
Looking for long-term relationship
5'9"
College degree
From Woodlands, Texas

I am impressed a man admitted he is five foot nine—most round up, adding at least two inches. However,

Kerry, you are just a little too young for Clare.

Bryan, 29, Doctor, Houston
Bio: Focused, dedicated, and motivated. Traveling is part of
the lifestyle I live.
Looking for long-term relationship
5'11"
No kids, but wants kids
From Chicago, Illinois
Interests: Hiking, Traveling, Reading, Learning

Bryan has four perfectly curated photos on his profile. They show his face close up, his athletic body with all of his clothes on, his personality through an activity, and his dog. Physically he matches everything Clare said she was attracted to: taller than her, athletic build, light features, and pretty colored eyes. Swipe right.

Mitch, 25, League City
Bio: Looking for something easy to fill my time. Here for a
good time, not a long time!
Looking for something casual
Has kids

From Alvin, Texas

Mitch has one photo with three children. I think it's safe to say, all of them are his. Clare is open to someone who already has kids, but I think three might be a little too many, especially since Mitch is only 25. Also, in this particular picture, it's hard to even see what he really looks like. Swipe left.

Detective Oliver

My phone vibrates, almost falling off the side of my desk. How did it even get so close to the edge? That's not where it's supposed to go.

"Detective Oliver." I always answer the phone the same, even if I can see who it is.

"Detective," Liam states and takes a deep breath.

"What's up, Liam? Where are you?"

"Finishing up a run." I check the clock. It's almost one in the afternoon. Liam often spends lunch time running. Since he's on call most of the time, he has to figure out little pockets of time to fit the rest of his life in.

"I just got a call," Liam pauses again. He always knows how to build suspense. "They identified the second body."

"Oh?" I wonder why no one called me yet and pleasantly surprised it didn't take long at all.

"Wait? You didn't get the report?"

"I'm confused, Liam. Didn't you call to tell me about it?"

"No, not exactly." He takes more deep breaths. "I thought they sent over the report?"

A little impatiently, I say, "I haven't received anything."

"Oh. I haven't either. I just looked at my emails. I haven't gotten a report, but Casey called me, I guess he was just excited to tell me."

"I'll just wait on the report to come through."

"His name was Tony Aaron Jones."

I nod and grab a pen writing down the name on my note pad.

"I'm heading back now."

Liam still believes the two bodies found in the bayou are connected and the result of something sinister. I know something is off here, but I'm not ready to make the same leap.

I type Tony's full name into the system. Page after page slowly loads—looks like Tony might have a longer criminal history than Tomas did. I'll be here reading this a while.

"Oh," James says as he walks in the house. He kisses me and says, "I didn't expect you home so early."

"I know. I wasn't feeling the best, so I left a little early today."

"Love, what's the matter? What can I get you?" He hugs and kisses me again.

"Nothing. I am feeling better now."

"I feel like you have been getting sick a lot lately. Maybe we should make an appointment with the doctor?"

"I'm fine, I really am. Why don't you go put your stuff away and meet me in the living room."

James does as he's told while I finish up in the kitchen. Ten minutes later, we meet in the living room.

"What's this?"

James looks at the tray I set on the coffee table. On the tray sits his favorite cocktail, a cup of hot ginger tea, and a baby bottle. James looks at me, confused, and back to the tray. Eye brows furrowed, back at me and the tray again.

"Wait." He finally says, bending down picking up the other thing on the tray—the positive pregnancy test. "Is this for real?"

Tears fall from my eyes as I shake my head. His mouth falls open first, not in fear, but in disbelief. Then the smile hits, slow at the edges, growing until it takes over his whole face. He pulls me into him, wrapping me in his arms. Tears fall from my eyes as I shake my head. James immediately wraps me in his arms.

"I can't believe it!"

"Me either," I whisper. "And you were right, we have an appointment with the doctor next week."

James picks up his cocktail and hands me my tea. We cheers.

"To our baby."

"To baby Oliver."

"Ohmygosh. We have to come up with a name that goes with Oliver." I let out a low, exaggerated groan and crumble into James's arms. He kisses me.

"Oh, baby. We have time for all of that."

I tell him Ashley was the one who put the idea in my head to take the test and how I nearly lost it in the bathroom at work.

"Why did you take it at work?" He asks, simply out of curiosity.

"I just HAD to know!"

We cheers again, taking a moment to process, both taking long gulps of our drinks.

"I thought it wasn't possible?" He questions.

"Me either. I mean, that is what they told us."

"To the doctor's being wrong." We lift our glasses and cheers again.

"A baby, huh?" He smiles at me and that becomes the phrase he repeats the rest of the night.

"A baby!" I repeat.

We cheers again and again. I tell him why I took the test in the first place and how crazy it is that it actually happened for us. We sit in the peace and the joy for the rest of the evening.

"You are in a good mood this morning." Liam almost questions my mood.

"I am." I give him a smile and nothing else. James and I agreed we would wait to tell anyone about the baby until we see a doctor and ensure everything is healthy.

"Okay." Liam states, seemingly annoyed. "I.T. got into Tomas's computer."

"What did they find on it?"

"Honestly, not a lot. The man watched a lot of porn."

"That tracks. Any emails that might lead to someone wanting to harm him?"

"No. Nothing that even suggested he had enemies or was into anything sinister."

Other than all the women he hurt.

I didn't really think there would be a lot found on his computer. Sometimes people have crazy search histories, but also, if Tomas was killed, he's the victim, not a murderer.

"We have a subpoena for his cell phone company for access to his records." Liam looks back at his notes. "Oh, we did get access to credit card records. His last purchase was at The Wild Hare."

He hands me a print out of the credit card statement. Highlighted at the top is a single charge for $56 at The Wild Hare dated almost a month ago.

"Where is The Wild Hare?"

Liam types the name into this computer and we both watch as it loads showing a small bar located right off the Buffalo Bayou. We give each other the knowing look—the look that says this must have been the night he went into the water.

"It doesn't open until two. We can head there then?" Liam asks.

I nod and head back to my office. If this was the last place Tomas visited and then went into the bayou that night, that means he was in the water for weeks just like Ashley suggested.

In my office, I go through the rest of Tomas's credit card charges. I find the typical expenses: food, gas, groceries. As I continue to comb through the file, I see an expense for a place I never heard of before. A quick search told me, Tomas paid for a premium subscription to a dating site. The expense was charged monthly, I assume an automatic withdraw.

EVEN AT TWO IN the afternoon, the bar is dimly lit. It's a small place, tucked behind big cypress trees right next to the bayou. I probably have driven by it and never knew it was back here.

"I saw a charge on the credit card statement for a dating site. What are the chances he was on a date that night?" I say to Liam while we are waiting for the bar manager to make his way to the front to speak with us.

"Oh, good catch. I didn't even see that charge." Liam says and starts looking around the bar. He's searching the walls for cameras—something I did as soon as we set foot in the place, too.

"Have you ever been here?" I ask Liam. He shakes his head.

"Hi, I'm Shawn. The manager." A tall, thin blonde haired man appears in front of me and Liam. We introduce ourselves and explain why we are here today.

Shawn clicks around on a computer behind the bar for few minutes. "Yup. Looks like a Tomas Mark was charged for four spicy margaritas on that day. So unless someone stole and used his card, he was in here. And left no tip." He rolls his eyes.

"Can you tell me who was working that night? We will want to question them."

"Of course. Let me pull that up." He clicks around a few more times before telling us he was not working that evening, but there were two bartenders working the bar while two waiters were working the tables. Only one of them is currently in the bar working today.

"It looks like it was a slow night. The owner was here too." Shawn says.

"Who is the owner?" Liam asks while jotting down names.

"His name is Harry. He should be here soon."

"We'll stick around to talk to him too." I nod at Liam.

"Are there any cameras?" I ask.

Shawn grimaces. "Not in the bar. I believe there's one outside the front door."

"Hmm."

Of course, it would make our job almost obsolete if there were cameras set up everywhere—but also that might be some kind of invasion of privacy; Big Brother watching and all that. As a private citizen, I understand, but as a cop, it would make my job easier.

Liam heads over to Katherine, the bartender who was working the night Tomas was in. I let him handle the conversation and I head back out the front door. Looking up, there is a camera, but it doesn't look very reliable. Walking around to the back of the building, I see only one other door—it says its for employees only and is locked.

To the right of the small building, is a set of stairs. I walk down them. As expected, they lead directly to the bayou. The walking path follows the twists of the bayou. The water is flowing and the current is strong. There's no fence or barrier between the walking path and the water—just a few feet drop. Anyone could stumble down here and fall right in. Honestly, I'm surprised that doesn't happen more often than it does. It's been a while since a body was discovered in the bayou and that was ruled an accident—this might just be another accident.

I meet Liam at the front of the bar and he introduces me to Harry, a medium-build dark skin man dressed in a button-up complete with suspenders. He looks like he just walked out of the 1920s.

"It's nice to meet you, Harry." I extend my hand. "This is a quaint little place you have."

"Thank you. Would either of you like something to drink?" He asks.

Both Liam and I laugh.

"Thanks, but we are definitely on the clock right now." Liam says.

"Oh, of course."

"Does the camera out front work?" I ask, getting straight to business.

"Liam was telling me what's going on. I will have to check the system. Unfortunately, it doesn't always capture everything or save everything." He sighs. "It's the weirdest thing. I need to look into getting something new and better. We didn't have a large budget when we first opened. This was all we could afford and hoped it would work as more of a deterrent."

"Shawn said you were working that night. Did you see Tomas Mark here?" I show him a picture that I have saved to my phone. It is a picture of Tomas we pulled off his computer—dated the night he was at the bar.

Harry studies the photo, taking my phone in his hand. "He doesn't look familiar. I am normally good with faces, but if he's only been in here the one night, I wouldn't really recognize him."

I take my phone and exhale slowly.

"I'm sorry." Harry says. "I wish I could help more."

"It will help if you can get the camera footage to us as soon as possible."

"Of course. I will do that right now."

"Thank you, Harry." Liam says. Harry says goodbye and disappears behind bar door.

"What did Katherine have to say?" I turn to Liam.

He shakes his head and starts walking toward the parking lot. "She wasn't any help either."

Tomas was here that night, but no one seems to remember him.

As we start walking toward the car, I point to the side of the building; Liam's gazes over.

"There's stairs back there. Leads right to the bayou." I tell him.

"Hmm."

"He might have stumbled down there after getting drunk here and accidentally went into the water."

"That's one theory." I think Liam might be so excited to be on his first potential murder case that he wants it to be more than a drunken accident.

"What's another theory?"

"I don't know. But a few margaritas won't get a man of Tomas's size drunk. Definitely not drunk enough to stumble to his death."

"Valid. We don't know if he only had that to drink that night. He could have drank before he made it to the bar and he had all those pills, there's no telling what was in his system." Liam nods along. "We still haven't received the toxicology report from Ashley."

"You're right. We'll wait for that." Deflated, Liam drives back to the station.

As we walk into the station, Aida frantically stops us before I can get back to my office.

"Tony's sister is here!" She says.

"Okay?" I raise my eyebrow at her reaction.

"She is not okay." Aida says, pointing to the conference room. His sister is pacing around, burning a hole in the carpet.

I shake my head.

"I can handle this." Liam says.

"No, it's okay. I'll go check it out." Before I go into the conference room, I make my way to my office and set my stuff down.

"About time! Someone called me saying my brother is dead!" A petite, dark haired, tattoo'd woman runs up to me. I take a step back—because I'm afraid of what she might suddenly do and how I might have to react.

"Ma'am. Have a seat." On second thought, I really should have let Liam take this one. She doesn't listen, remaining standing in front of me.

"I'm Detective Grace Oliver. Can you tell me what your name is?"

"I'm Britt Jones. Tony is my brother. I got a call that his body was found." Her voice is raised and shaky.

I motion for her to sit; this time, she does and I sit across from her. I assume Aida took the woman's identification to verify who she is claiming to be.

"Yes, Britt. Tony's body was found in the Buffalo Bayou."

"Dead?"

"Yes, ma'am. I am so sorry."

"How?"

"We are unsure at this time."

"Are you trying to find out?" The anger in her voice is loud and clear.

"Yes, of course we are."

"What are you doing to find out?"

"Well, I'm glad you are here today. I would like to ask you some questions."

She rolls her eyes. "I guess that's okay."

Britt tells me she hasn't seen her brother in almost a year and I wonder why she is so distraught about him being found dead. She says a lot of words without saying much, very fast. Then, she starts explaining their complicated relationship.

"Can you file charges on a dead person?" She asks.

I look at her confused. "What kind of charges?"

"Rape." Her fist form balls.

I want to reach out to her. "Britt," I keep my voice calm and words slow. "Did Tony rape you?"

She shakes her head. A single tear drops to the table. She wipes it away. "I guess that bastard got what was coming to him."

"I am so sorry that you had to go through that."

Liam opens the door interrupting us.

"I'm sorry, Detective, can I speak with you?" Liam asks. I nod and follow him out the door.

"What's up, Liam?" I ask.

"Nothing. Just figured I would give you a minute to breathe."

"Thanks. Add Britt to our suspect list for Tony."

"What?" He genuinely looks shocked.

"She was just telling me about how he raped her. She seems relieved he is dead."

"Oh boy."

Liam follows me back into the room with Britt. We explain that we would like to ask her more questions but want the session to be recorded.

"Am I a suspect now? Oh, god." Panic sets in.

"We are still trying to gather all evidence. It seems like you have a motive. So we would like to find out more. Of course, if you would like a lawyer present, you have every right to call one." I explain.

She sighs. "Yea, like I just have a lawyer to call. I don't have anything to hide."

Britt willingly shows us her phone and gives us detailed lists of where she has been and what she has been doing the last few months. She provides people who can verify all of the information she has provided. It is a lot for us to go through, but we have to ensure Britt wasn't the person who caused Tony to go into the bayou. The accident angle we are working with for Tomas could be the same for Tony as well; unfortunately, we haven't been able to rule anything out or in for either case.

Madison

Beep. Beep. Beep.

"Hey guys! It's been too long since I made an update video! I just wanted to again say I have been so blown away by all the support and messages I have received. I can only take on one client at a time, so it's going to still take me some time to get through all the messages. I am happy to report my first client has had success and happily dating a man I set her up with. I am currently working with another client with hopes of finding her a great match as well. I am loving being able to help in this way and will continue to do so! Much love!"

I post the video labeling it 'Ghost Dating Update! #ghostdater.'

Did I just lie about Layla? That gut feeling hits again. I haven't heard from her this week; I hope everything is okay and make a note to check in with her soon.

Message from Mark:

Hey, how are you?

Hey! I'm great! How are you?

Message from Landon:

You are so beautiful and sexy af. Let's get to know each other let me know how you pose to be treated.

What kind of message is that, Landon? I delete the conversation.

Message from Bryan:

Good afternoon, Clare. I see you own a Pilates studio. How did you get into that? I tried Pilates once and it was a great workout, but I generally stick to lifting and running.

Good afternoon Bryan. I own 2 studios now. I started practicing years ago and loved it, so I decided to make it my career. *smile emoji*

Message from Greg:

You are absolutely stunning. *heart eyes emoji* If your personality is as beautiful as your pictures let's meet up, get to know each other, and explore the possibility of us. Hope to hear from you soon. Sincerely, Greg.

I don't know how to feel about that message from Greg. I click back on his profile, wondering why I even swiped right in the first place. His profile says he is 28 but looks more like he is in his late thirties. It also says he is looking for something casual—Clare is looking for something more serious, so clearly that was a mistake on my part. I delete the conversation, unmatching Clare and Greg.

ELLIE'S FACE IS BEAMING as soon as I answer the video call. I wonder what she is so excited about, but don't immediately ask. I am sitting at my desk that is pushed up against the wall with the window in my bedroom. When I sit here, the chair touches the bed. The tollway fines, car registration, and medical bills I am shifting through tell me I won't be able to get a bigger apartment any time soon.

"Hey, Madison!" Ellie says, I believe for the second time.

"Hey," I say with a sigh.

"What's wrong?"

I put my unpaid bills in the drawer, so I can forget about them a little while longer. "Oh, nothing."

"I don't believe you for one second. You forgot how well I know you." Ellie always pays attention to my emotions and asks me about them—she is one of the only people, correction, she *is* the only person I actually open up to. I shake my head to shake off her question.

"How was your doctor's appointment this morning?" She finally asks.

"It was fine. You know, just a check up."

"I know but I worry every time you have to go in. When will you get the test results?"

I roll my eyes. "Don't worry about me, mom!" I say acting like an annoyed teenager—although I never actually got to be one. "They should come back in about a week."

"Don't roll your eyes at my young lady!" She laughs at herself. "I know, I know. How have you been feeling, physically? Any illness as of late?"

I shake my head, not being able to lie to her out loud. Have I been experiencing symptoms? Was the heavy, long period two months in a row normal or a symptom? I don't even know how to tell anymore.

Ellie lowers her gaze away from the phone camera. "Let me know the results as soon as you know."

"Enough about nothing. You seemed super excited when I answered the call. What's happening?"

She looks back into the camera, her eyes light back up. "Oh yea!" She sits up and adjusts herself on her bed. "I got the promotion!"

Ellie has been working at the same company since we graduated, slowly working her way up the corporate ladder. This promotion means she will be a senior manager.

"Ellie! Congrats! That's amazing!" You deserve it, you have been working so hard."

She smiles again, because she knows she deserves everything she has, including her amazing husband, beautiful baby girl, and another little girl on the way.

"I don't know how you do it all. But does this mean you won't be able to come down any time soon?" I ask selfishly.

"I know. I feel like a terrible friend, since I haven't been down there in so long. I will soon, I promise!"

"I'm only teasing. I need to come up there too. We are both bad friends."

After a few moments of silence, Ellie asks, "How is the ghost dating going?"

"It's been good actually. Layla and Tony are still dating and that seems...well, I haven't heard from her in a while actually." That feeling pierces my stomach again.

"That's great, but it's only been a few weeks though, right?"

"Yea."

"But that's amazing. Good job, Madison."

"Did I tell you I took on another client?" She shakes her head, so I fill her in on Clare.

"That's great. I'm glad you started doing something like this. It really suits you and I think you are really helping people. And I'm sure you've got a long line waiting on your services."

I nod. "Yea, I kind of do." I smile, a little bit of pride washes over me, an unusual feeling.

"Well, that's great. I am going to let you get to your dating."

"Okay! Give Nick and Jess love for me."

"I will." She blows a kiss at the phone. "Love you."

"Love you."

I OPEN UP THE dating application. Anxiety creeps in, then I remember I am not searching through these profiles for myself. I love finding significant others for other people, but trying to find someone for myself would be anxiety-inducing—which is why I gave up years ago. I take five deep breaths and continue reading messages to Clare.

Message from Mark:

> I'm great! Thanks for asking. I can see from your profile you are beautiful entrepreneur. So clearly you got great dreams and the ability to accomplish them. What is one dream you haven't yet accomplished yet.

> Thank you *smile emoji* Hmm..a dream I haven't accomplished? I really want to write a book one day. What about you? What is a dream you have yet to accomplish?

Message from Jonathan:

> That is awesome. Maybe I can come take a class sometime. And maybe I can take you on a hike sometime. Well the most of one we can in Houston.

> Yea…maybe…where do you like to go hike here?

I tap on Mark's picture to open up his profile to review it again.

Mark, 27, Self-employed, Houston
Bio: Fun, spontaneous, down to earth
Looking for long-term relationship
6'
No kids, but wants kids
From Denver, Colorado
Interests: Running, Skiing, Stand-up Comedy, Dogs, TV &
Movies

He has five pictures; three of them are just of his face. I generally hate when men only post selfies, however he has piercing light brown eyes that I cannot stop staring at. One of the other pictures is a full-body image, but it was taken at a distance, so not only can I not see his body, he looks like an ant not a grown, tall man. The final picture is of his back and he is looking up at a waterfall—I will say it's a great picture, just not great for a dating profile. I don't know exactly how I feel about his profile or why I initially swiped right on him, nevertheless, the conversation is going in a good direction, so we will keep that one going a little while longer.

I click back to the liked section of the application: Clare had about 98 more likes—I start sifting through them, thinking I need Clare to be having more than just two conversations. Surely there is more than two decent men in Houston that match what Clare is looking for.

King, 23, Portland
Bio: Hey ther

That's it. That's the profile. There is one picture of King's face with a hat and sunglasses on. Do men get matches with minimal information and pictures?! Clearly he is active on the application, since he sent Clare a like. I shake my head and swipe left.

Ig, 27, Actor, Houston
Bio: Message to fine out, no one reads these anyway.
6'

Ig's first photo is a group of three guys and one girl—which one are you Ig? I keep scrolling and there are three other photos of cats. Swipe left.

Ave, 32, Scientist, Houston

Bio: Athletic INFP. A male with curly black hair, girl dad x3, 50-50 custody, amicable divorced for years. Gardener of rare trees, yogi, rescue cat/dog dad. Funny and fun. 1/3 nerd, 1/3 artist, 1/3 jock. Enter at your own risk.
Looking for casual

This is where I stop. The first photo is of Ave and I will admit, he is a good looking man and fits the physical description Clare goes for normally. However, again, Clare is looking for long-term relationship potential—which is clearly displayed on her profile. Why like someone that isn't looking for the same thing you are?

Val, 34, Server, Houston
Bio: Reserved...no dinners, no scammers, no strippers, no hustlers. Not interested in text back and forth. If you too busy meet, don't bother. Not in BBW.
5'10"
No kids, wants kids
From Nashville, Tennessee

I don't even know why I kept reading after 'no dinners,' what is that even about, Val? I don't look at his pictures, it's an immediate swipe left. I go through about 16 more profiles, just like this.

Okay, maybe there isn't a lot of great men in Houston. I exit the application. This one is presenting to be more of a challenge.

MY PHONE LIGHTS UP on my desk.

My stomach lurches. I never take personal calls at work, but this has to be important. I stumble getting my headphones in before the call disconnects.

"Layla?" I am almost whispering. There is rustling at the end of the phone and the screen is dark. "Where are you? Layla?"

I move to a conference room close to my desk for privacy—not that the floor to ceiling glass walls offer much privacy.

"Madison, yes." She is whispering and definitely in a closet. "I need your help."

"What's going on?"

"It's Tony."

My heart drops to my stomach. "Layla, what's going on?" I ask a little too impatiently.

Layla finally starts spilling everything. After their second date, Tony basically invited himself over to her house and never left. He would show up everyday after work with more clothes that he said he just brought from his house, however, she never saw his house and found price tags in the bathroom trash can for all of the clothes. She said she didn't think anything at first, because it was fun and exciting and she liked having a man around the house.

"He was great. We would cook together. He would take out the trash. Things were great..." her voice trails.

"Until they weren't." I finish her sentence. "It's only been a few weeks, Layla. What is he doing to you?"

"A few days ago, he started turning off the WiFi at the house, so I couldn't access the internet while I was with him. He would go through my phone when I got home to make sure I wasn't talking to other men throughout the day." She puts her hand on her head in exhaustion.

"I feel so stupid, I let him do this, because I had nothing to hide. But he never believed me and just keeps getting more and more jealous."

"Please don't feel stupid."

"Then...he got physical with me. I had a few bruises. I've never dealt with this before. I don't know what to do. They were still visible, I had to cancel plans with my family." She starts sobbing.

"Is he still at your house?"

"Yes. I asked him to leave. And he refused."

My face grows hot. "What?! He refused to leave your house?!"

She shakes her head. "He said he has no place to go right now." She pauses. "His apartment complex sold or changed owners or something, so they kicked everyone out." She hears what she just said. "Do you think that is even true? Oh God. I'm so stupid."

"Yes, that's definitely a lie." My head is spinning and I'm pacing the room. How do I even help her? He needs to get out of her house at the very least.

"I don't know what to do."

"Can you do me a favor?"

She finally wipes away the tears. "Anything."

"I need any and all information you can find out about him. Old address, driver's license number, anything. I couldn't find much when I searched his number, but if I have more information, I can find out more."

"I can try. He's pretty guarded. But he did bring in a box that looked like it might have some of that kind of stuff in it."

"Just try, and be careful."

She nods. "Thank you, Madison. I knew you could help me."

"I am so sorry you are in this situation. And I feel like I put you here. I am so, so sorry." I lower my head—this is all my fault and I need to fix it now.

"You couldn't have known either. And I rushed into things with a stranger. I feel so dumb."

"Please don't feel guilty either. This is on him, not you."

We hang up and the guilt washes over me. I cannot believe I didn't uncover any signs of this behavior before I set Layla up with Tony. Normally, I see these signs, however, I didn't see this coming.

"Is everything okay?" Robbie asks when he sees me coming out of the conference room. I shake my head as I walk back to my desk. He follows.

"One of the guys I set a client up with is acting...um...funny." I didn't want to say too much, or anything at all.

"Oh. Hm. Sorry to hear that?"

I sigh.

"Didn't you look him up before you set her up?"

How dare he question my process. "Of course I did! Everything checked out."

"What about the group on Facebook?"

I unclench my jaw and look up at him, confused.

"Girl! The "Are We Dating the Same Guy" group? How have you not heard of this?"

How had I never heard of this? I grab my phone again, click open Facebook, search the group—there's a ton of these groups, all over the country. I click the Houston one and hit join. I have to wait on approval before I can see what has been posted, since it's a private group. Apparently, it is a place where women post pictures of men they are involved with or starting to get to know; other women then comment on their experience with that man. A warning system of sorts. Women banding together, helping each other, saving one another from the monsters of this world.

Detective Oliver

I SAVE VERY DETAILED notes with the interview transcript with Britt to my computer under Tony's file. So far, her story is adding up; Aida is checking on some key details. We still don't have an accurate date Tony might have went into the water; I make a mental note to head down to see Ashley soon.

An email pulls my attention before I could write down that mental note. I click on it and Tomas's phone records and dating profile start downloading. Before it can finish, Liam is at my door.

"Did you see the email?" He asks, eagerly.

I nod. "Just opening it."

When the files download, I extend my computer screen to the large television in my office. Liam takes a seat in a small, leather chair—I realize the furniture was just placed in this office, I had no say over what was included. Liam opens up his notebook, ready to take notes.

I start with the phone call log—which doesn't reveal much information. It looks like the only calls Tomas received were from spam numbers. He only had a handful of outgoing calls; those being to his bank, his landlord, and his mother. His mother had said she hadn't seen or heard from him in about six months when he called asking about money, but they talked on the phone for about 20 minutes three months ago. She might have just had her timeline a little off; we will verify with her about that again.

Liam laughs, while I'm highlighting parts of the call log and making a note to follow up.

"What's funny?" I ask, shooting him a look.

"You always start with the call log. These are millennials. They don't talk on the phone."

He's right, but I'm also a millennial and I talk on the phone all the time—I don't like when people make assumptions based on when someone was born. I click over to the text message log—hundreds of pages populate. Since this is an active case that's possibly a homicide, we were able to obtain full text message receipts. Clicking through these messages, we find a short list of potential suspects.

"Stop." Liam holds up his hand pointing at the screen. "Click on Clare's name."

I do as he asks. A few messages between Tomas and Clare fill the screen. Clare and Tomas appear to have made plans to meet up at The Wild Hare.

"Bingo. She must have been the reason he was there that night. Let's get her information and get to questioning her."

Most of Tomas's texts were about work and obtaining drugs from his friends. Maybe they weren't his friends and just his drug dealers. Most of them let him down though, not having whatever he was looking to get high with.

Finally, I click over to the dating application information. Again, we were able to obtain full details easily. Normally, companies drag out this process, even with warrants and subpoenas. Thankfully, they didn't fight too hard to maintain their member's privacy, this time.

Tomas has sent hundreds of disgusting messages to dozens of women. The only name that matches from the dating application to his text messages was Clare. Surprisingly, the messages to Clare are clean and appropriate. Probably why she agreed to meet him.

"Were you ever on this dating app?" I ask Liam.

He scoffs, shaking his head. "No, I wasn't on any dating app."

"Good," I let out a sigh of relief. But curiosity hits. "How did you meet your girlfriend, then?"

"Through friends." I nod at his response. Liam and I don't talk much about our personal lives, but we know some basics about each other.

"I'll have Aida look up this Clare." Liam says. "She might be the last person to see our boy."

"You are right. Let's talk to some of these other people Tomas texted. But focus on finding her first."

James greets me at the door with a bear hug. Flowers and an unopened bottle of wine sit on the dining room table.

"Oh shit. I'm such an idiot," he says, dramatically hitting himself in the forehead.

"Don't talk about my best friend like that!" I give him another hug.

"I wanted to celebrate and keep celebrating. I bought this wine, not even thinking. You can't have it!" He hits himself on the forehead. I laugh.

"It's okay, love. You can enjoy it. I'll have some tea and still celebrate along with you. Something smells delish." I say, looking around to the kitchen.

He runs to the oven, throwing it open. "Oh, thank god I didn't ruin that too."

"Oh, please don't be so hard on yourself."

"You are right." He shakes his body, as if to shake off the funk.

James pulls the food out of the oven and plates it. I make some tea and we sit next to each other at the table.

"How is your case going?" James asks.

A tired breath drifts past my lips.

"That bad, huh?"

"Not exactly. It's just there's a lot to go through, lots of unknowns. And we have two bodies. They could be related, or unrelated. Either could be accidents or not." I shrug.

"You said you had a feeling about it after the first one. What's your feeling now?"

"Still can't define it. But it's not good." I laugh, before taking a bite of food.

"What?" James laughs as well. unsure what he's laughing at.

"Maybe that feeling was just the baby?" We both laugh, because it could be true. Neither of us have done this before, we don't know what to do or how it should feel.

"Maybe. Or maybe it's just your spidey sense you have always had about these things." He puts his hand on mine.

"You might be right. We'll see. I am surprised at how cooperative most everyone has been, so far."

"What do you mean?"

"Normally it takes a long time to get things like phone records and such, but the phone companies acted fast." I pause to eat more. "Even, the dating application one of the victims had an active account, was fast in getting us records."

"That's good." James says, while clearing his plate.

I wrap up the evening by washing the dishes, like I always do. James makes me another cup of ginger tea and sets out a few chocolate covered almonds and berries.

"Want some ice cream too?" He asks.

I shake my head and he takes our after dinner snacks to the living room.

"THIS TIME START WITH the text messages." Liam teases.

We received Tony's phone records about an hour ago. I roll my eyes at him but click over to the text messages, first. His last message was from a Layla. I click to open the thread.

"Hmmm." Liam makes a noise. "Scroll up a little." I do as he asks. We keep, silently reading messages.

"Looks like she invited him out and was running late. What's that address?"

Liam already was searching the address Layla had sent over to Tony. He gasps. "The Wild Hare."

"Oh." I don't know what else to say.

I keep scrolling through the messages. These messages asking to meet at the bar that night, are the first in a few weeks from Layla. Before this date and group of messages, seems like they were meeting for the first time and getting to know each other only a few weeks ago.

I exit out of those messages and go to the next person on the list of texts; also labeled as coming from a Layla. I open and we start reading. It appears Layla and Tony started dating a few weeks ago and possibly moved in together—that seems fast, but I don't have much room to talk. Mine and James's relationship took shape quickly according to some people's standards.

"Why does he have two numbers for Layla?" Liam questions.

"No clue. Maybe she got a new one after they started dating? We will have to look into that."

"Looks like we also need to head back to The Wild Hare." Liam states; I nod.

"And we have another girlfriend to find."

"I told you these cases are definitely connected. Two men ended up in the bayou, one after another, both last at the same bar. It's too much of a coincidence."

"Again, let's follow the evidence. But, you might be right."

Liam smiles. "Say that again?"

I laugh. "Not a chance," I tease.

"I am going to keep going through these messages to see what else I can find and who else we need to question." I say.

"I'm going to go do the same. I'll have Aida try to find Layla. She's working on finding Clare."

"The phone number didn't help find her?" I hadn't been updated on Tomas's case.

He shakes his head. "It was one of those alternative numbers. We have to get another subpoena for them to release information."

People can sign up for additional phone numbers, so they don't have to give their real one out to strangers—this makes our job more challenging, as we have to contact another company to release information.

I sigh. There's always something holding us back and I thought things were moving fast and easily for us on this one. Things don't happen as quickly as they are portrayed on crime television shows.

"Let's head over to the bar at 2pm again. I'll make sure Harry will be there. He still owes us that video footage of Tomas." Liam stands to leave my office. I nod and make a note in my calendar.

I keep scrolling through Tony's phone records. It doesn't seem like he has many friends, contact with his family, or even a job. In deleted messages, I find a lot of other women he was connected to. These messages went from charming and sweet, to angry and controlling. A few women accusing him of cheating and owing them money. Some of the things the women accuse Tony of, just might make me sick—I can't wait until I'm out of the first trimester and over this nausea.

HARRY GREETS US OUTSIDE the bar; we say hello and pleasantries.

"I was actually just about to send over the footage I found." He says.

"Great! So you did find Tomas on the camera?" Liam asks.

Harry nods. "The camera outside the door caught him walking in, alone and then out with a woman."

Liam and I exchange looks. "Did you also include the footage of the woman walking into the bar?"

He shakes his head. "I couldn't find any. It is the oddest thing." He runs his fingers through his hair. "That's what was taking me so long to get it over to you. I had a few others scouring the footage as well. We never saw her walk in. Only have her walking out with Tomas, so you can only see the back of her head."

I sigh. "It looks like we will need you to go through some more footage for us. We had another body turn up in the bayou and the man's last known whereabouts is your bar as well."

"Shit." Harry turns to face the bar and then back to us. "Are you serious?! That's just a crazy coincidence, right?"

"We are trying to figure that out."

I can see Harry's mind racing. He's going through every picture in his head of every patron he's ever served; he's going through every interaction his employees have had.

"No, no, no." He finally says out loud.

"Sir?" Liam asks.

"Oh. Sorry." Harry offers no more. He walks into the bar and we follow.

Liam shows Harry and the employees here today a picture of Tony. As expected no one recognizes him or remembers if he was here with anyone the night he went into the water.

"Harry is going to send over footage for both nights and the list of people working and in the bar the night Tony went missing. I'll see who was here both nights and see if there is any other connection between the two men." I nod along, Liam is a good detective.

"What if this wasn't the last place they were, they just didn't use their cards again and went in the bayou later, so there's no actual connection to this place." He starts thinking out loud. I smile.

"Now you are really thinking like a detective. Always question everything until evidence points you in the right direction." I motion for him to follow me. "However, on this one, I might disagree."

"Really?" He knows I have been trying to find any reason to disconnect these two cases.

"Yea." I lead him behind the bar. "Look at how close this place is the bayou." We walk down the stairs.

"Oh damn. Yea. It was be super easy. Have a drink or many up at the bar, stumble down here, fall in the water."

I start looking around more closely than I had before. Looking around for any evidence of people down here, of an accident, of a struggle—anything.

"Let's get some help down here to look for any evidence that might have been left by anyone that might have been down here either night."

Liam stares off into the water. It's rushing again.

"All this rain, I bet we won't find much. You think there's any other bodies in the water?" Liam asks.

"Good question. We'll see if Joe wants to get a team out here to check."

Madison

I POSTED A PICTURE of Tony an hour ago on the Facebook group. Looking at my phone, I've missed a lot of notifications. I open the application and there's 63 comments. I audibly gasp.

"Oh, no. This isn't going to be good."

Comments:

Ana: He comes off as charming at first, states pure long-term dating intentions and starts a relationship quickly. Then begins accusing the women of seeing other men and being on dating apps while he gets caught in his own lie. These lies range from who is with to where he going.

Bri: He owes me $3,000. I stupidly loaned him money to fix his car. Should have known I would never have seen that money again. I dated him off and on for almost a year. We were exclusive the whole time though. Or so I though. Discovered he was with at least two other women while we were on and who knows how many while we were off.

Tiffani: I think I was the other woman to one of his 'serious' relationships. I didn't know he was in any relationship at the time, he told me he wanted to be exclusive with only me. Once I found out he was in a relationship I confronted him, of course he denied it, but I left right away.

Lisa: I'm friends with his most recent ex and been around them in many settings. He took in her kids and played Mr. Nice Guy. But after so many issues of theft, lies, and manipulation they broke up like 3 months ago. At one point he became physical with her. Be careful because he's really good at his lies from what I've seen of him.

Laura: Listen ladies...I dated this man and he was always cheating on me. I caught him messaging three other women constantly on every since social media platform and I always caught him in lies about what he was doing. He manipulates me in every way possible and still messages me to this day. This man will lie to your face and act like you're the crazy one.

Randi: Everything all these ladies are saying is true. I dated him for many years. I'm sure a lot of the ladies commenting were dating him at the same time I was. He moved into my house after only a few months and promised me the world. He's great at spinning everything in his favor and making you believe it. I too supported him and he owes me a ton of money I will never see again. I knew about the women but he convinced me nothing ever happened. And that y'all were the problem. I know I was dumb and naive. One time I confronted him about the lies, he became violent. I was finally able to escape but had to move, change my number, etc. Stay away!

I feel physically sick. I want to cry, throw up, beat Tony to a pulp, and give all these ladies a hug. I cannot believe there is 57 more comments just like this—*who the hell is this man?*

I paid a website to find out more information on Tony. *Why didn't I do this to begin with?!* These women didn't even get into half of Tony's horrible history. I thought we paid our police to keep people like this off the streets?!

"Ellie, what do I do?" I am shaking again after reading all the comments about Tony—they doubled overnight.

"Girl, what can you do? You just need to help Layla get away from him. That's all."

"Ugh!" I sigh, loudly. "I know, but I hate that nothing can be done to stop this man. This is disgusting. The number he gave showed up under a different last name." Layla sent me pictures of three driver's licenses she found, each with a different last name.

"Yea, I'm not sure that's a crime though, Madison."

"Yes, but he is a criminal. He has a felony on his record. He's been arrested for domestic violence. SEVERAL times. And he did hit Layla!" I am almost yelling at this point.

"Wait. What?!" Ellie screeches. "Why didn't you lead with all that? What the hell?"

"I told you this man is a monster. He cannot go near another woman again!"

"Madison, is Layla still at her home with him?" Ellie asks, calmly.

I nod my head. *Oh, shit.* Layla is still experiencing the hell brought on by this asshole right now.

"I need to help her get rid of him!"

"Yes, help her get away from his as soon as possible. You might have to get a restraining order from the sounds of it."

I nod again, although I have no plans of involving the authorities. From experience, they don't always take care of the problem appropriately; nor do they typically listen to women and believe their experiences.

"Keep me updated and be safe." Ellie ends the video call, leaving me to ponder on how to handle the situation.

You don't actually have to do anything, Madison. It's not exactly your problem.

Detective Oliver

I BOUNCE MY LEFT leg up and down, waiting on the doctor to finally come in the tiny examination room.

"Honey, relax." James grabs my hand, but drops it and wipes away my sweat.

"Easy for you to say." I shoot him a look.

"I'm nervous here too." He takes my hand again.

I lower my gaze. "I know. I'm sorry. I just want this to be it for us. We deserve it, right?"

"Yes," he kisses my forehead. "We do. Babe, whatever happens, we are in this together."

I nod and open my mouth to speak as a knock on the door startles me.

"Hi! Grace, you are definitely pregnant. The test confirms it."

"Yes, but is everything okay with the baby?" My leg continues to bounce.

"I'm sending you down for an ultrasound. That will tell us how far along you are and if everything at this point looks normal."

I almost scoff at the word 'normal.' *What is normal?*

"You told us we couldn't get pregnant. Is there any reason to believe this pregnancy won't be viable?" James asks.

"Did the nurse tell you we will also take some blood today?" I shake my head. "Good. We are going to order some tests." The doctor scribbles lines on a piece of paper attached to my hefty file. "But right now, I don't see why this won't be a successful pregnancy."

I let out the breath I didn't know I was holding. Just her saying those words, makes me feel infinitely better.

We ask a few more questions about what we should be doing to ensure a healthy pregnancy and baby. Typical answers were given, plenty of water, a balanced diet, reduced stress. We all laugh knowing my job will always be stressful.

It's been twenty minutes since we walked from the doctors office on the third floor of the medical building, down to the first floor. The doctor ordered an ultrasound, but there was a few expecting parents waiting before it was our turn. I watch as woman and woman walk out of the ultrasound room, smiling holding images of their growing babies. I grab James's hand a little tighter.

"Oliver?" The doctor calls our last name, we stand, and follow her into the small, dimly lit room.

"I'm Sophia. I will be doing your ultrasound today."

"Nice to meet you." James says and shakes her hand; I'm unable to speak.

"Have you received a vaginal ultrasound before?"

I nod my head.

"Then you know the drill. I'll leave so you can get undressed from the waist down. You've exempted your bladder, right?"

I nod my head again. She leaves so I can get undressed in privacy, well my husband is still in the room. I always wondered why doctors leave the room, just for you to undress. I mean, they are still going to see everything anyway. Also, why do we—women—hide our underwear when, again, they are going to see everything anyway? *I mean, we all do this right?*

There's a knock at the door and Sophia comes back in the room. I'm laying on the paper covered table with a paper "sheet" draped over my legs. I had an ultrasound like this when we were doing tests to determine why we couldn't get pregnant. So I know what to expect, but it's not any more comfortable the second time.

"You'll feel pressure." There is a lot of pressure.

The pain, the uncomfortableness, the fear fade away as a small circle appears on the screen.

"Lub-dub. Lub-dub. Lub-dub."

"Is that the heartbeat?" I whisper.

"Yes. It sounds strong." Sophia says. "I'm going to take..."

I'm sure Sophia said more as she keeps moving the wand—whatever that thing is called—inside me, but I keep staring at my baby and listening to the heartbeat.

"Are you okay?" James asks. I'm still laying on the bed in the ultrasound room. I can't seem to move.

"Yea." I nod my head. "I just can't believe, James. We are having a baby." Tears roll down my face.

We get to take home the first images of our baby, although it looks like an alien.

Liam bursts through my office door. "Oh good! You are back!" He's out of breath.

I roll my eyes. "What is wrong Liam?"

He takes a moment. "There's a woman."

"What?"

"In the footage. With both men. There's a woman. The same woman."

"Okay?"

He points to my computer. "I just send you some stills."

I open my email and sure enough the last one is from Liam; the time stamp only 10 seconds ago—no wonder he is out of breath.

I project the image onto the computer screen. It's a side by side comparison of two still images. It's grainy, it's black and white, it's far away.

"That's Tony and some woman." Liam points to the left side. "And that's Tomas and the same woman." He points to the other image.

I study the images, not exactly seeing what Liam is seeing.

"I know. Click open the other images." I do as he says.

The next image is zoomed in closer. There's definitely a woman holding up each man as they exit the bar.

"See. They have the same build. The hair is obviously light. I wish we had a color video, but this is what we got. She's probably around five foot, five foot one. Light hair. Probably 130, 140 pounds."

Zoom out, and side-by-side, it does appear to be the same woman. Liam also could be accurate with his description. Based on the height of the men, while both slumped over on top of the woman, you can tell she is significantly shorter than them. He is probably estimating her weight based on her build and compared next to the men's weight.

"Do you have images of this woman entering the bar?"

Liam shakes his head. "It's like Harry said. There's absolutely no footage of her entering. I had him send me all of the footage from these days. I watched it three times. Each. There's no images of her entering."

"Does any of the employees fit the description?"

"No. Harry sent over all of the employees information and none of them match this description."

"Unless he didn't send over everyone?" I question.

"It's possible. But Aida compared payroll reports to the list. Unless he is paying someone else under the table. But we didn't give him the description of this woman."

"Well, he saw the footage before we did."

"Oh you are right. However, I don't know." He pauses. "I know. I need to keep questioning everything."

I nod and looking back at the images. *Who are you?*

"There is one thing." I look back at Liam. "Harry was definitely at the bar both nights." I raise my eyebrow. "That's not it. I don't think he was involved. I know, everyone is still a suspect right now."

"Every one is and no one is. We still don't have evidence of an actual crime."

"Yes. Anyway. He was there that night but one of the nights the camera shows him leaving the bar but never arriving."

"Well there is a back door. I assume for employees only."

"You'e right. There's a door. But he showed me the door doesn't open. From the inside or the outside."

"Are you sure?"

"I checked it myself."

I believe he checked it. It doesn't seem safe to have a back door that doesn't work. That is neither here nor there at this point. We need to figure out what happened to these men and quickly.

"We've got a team out at the bayou today." I tell Liam, as if he didn't already know.

"I've got Aida seeing if there are any patrons that was at the bar both nights."

I sigh and sit back down at my desk. We are no closer to figuring out what happened to Tony or Tomas.

Madison

I WAKE TO A text notification from Layla.

> I asked Tony to leave this morning.
> I have no idea where he stayed last
> night. He broke down crying that he
> loved me more than anything in this
> world and that he also just lost his job
> so he has nowhere to go or money. He
> got a little aggressive, so I backed off
> and left for work.

He wasn't entirely lying—he did lose his job, just months ago, not recently. His profile also made it seem like he has his own business, or a few, but this was clearly a lie, just one of many. In my research, I also found out he has been kicked out of his apartment about six months ago for failure of payment. I text Layla back immediately.

> Don't pressure him anymore. I don't want you getting hurt anymore. Find some place to stay for a few days please. Don't go back home. I'll take care of this. Trust me.

I am still logged into the phone number application I used as Layla when I first texted Tony.

Message to Tony:

> Hey babe! I am so sorry about this morning. Just a little self-sabotaging another relationship. I love you!

> Why are you using this number?

Shit Madison, of course Layla isn't using this fake number anymore. Think quick, three dots appear, Tony is typing another message.

> Oh silly me. I just came back to our initial conversations to remind myself why I fell in love with you in the first place *kissy face emoji*

> *kissy face emoji* Babe, I am sorry for getting a little aggressive this morning, it won't happen again. I just can't lose you and what we have. I love you more than anything in this world.

> I know. I want to do something special tonight. I'm going to send you a location, will you meet me there at 8p tonight?

> I'll meet you anywhere.

WALKING INTO THE BAR, I take a deep breath. I've never been here before, but the pictures online showed a small, dimly lit establishment—a perfect spot to not be noticed. It's also nestled among trees, hidden from the road. I spot Tony instantly. The man is prompt, I'll give him that. I take a seat to his left at the bar.

"Welcome in. What can I get started for you?" The petite red head behind the bar sets down a napkin for my anticipated drink.

"Hi, uh. I have never been here before. Let me take a look at the menu."

"Take your time, doll." She walks away to make other drinks.

I lean over close to Tony and his drink. "OH, what are you drinking?"

"Uh. Oh." He's taken aback; he didn't notice someone had sat next to him. "It's a, uh, gin and tonic."

"Oh, they made it look so fancy." I smile, trying my best to be friendly. "But I cannot handle my gin."

Is that a thing? Do people not handle their gin well? I never drank much—being off and on medications my whole life made having a "normal" life more challenging; that included drinking alcohol.

Tony makes a noise and then turns away from me to check his phone. The bright screen illuminates his face in this dark place. He is clearly looking for where Layla must be.

I called her after Tony agreed to meet me. I told her to block his number and delete all his information from her phone. However, I said to wait until later tonight to do so. She was a little suspicious but agreed.

Tony tried calling someone, but they don't answer—I thought he broke his phone the way he slammed it on the bar.

The bartender walks back over, concerned but not drawing attention to Tony's outburst. "What did you decide?" She's talking to me, but keeps glancing over at Tony.

"I think I'll just take the spicy margarita." I close the menu, I hadn't even read. "Can my new friend here get another gin and tonic?"

Tony grunted again. The bartender nods, raises her eyebrow as if to ask if I was sure, then turns to start making our drinks. I pull out my phone.

Message to Tony:

> Sorry, babe. Got caught up at work. Be there soon *kissy face emoji*

Tony picks up his phone immediately and sighs, putting it back down, gently this time.

"Your date standing you up like it seems mine is?" I try making small talk and sound light.

"No." His jaw clenches, he's triggered.

"Sorry."

Our drinks arrive and I pay cash for them. I lift my glass to his.

"Cheers," I smile weakly.

"Uh. Cheers." He says and then gulps over half the glass in one go.

I take a small sip of mine. I can't drink any more than that—I need a clear head. I watch as Tony excessively checks his phone and the door to the bar. He finally goes to stand. He stumbles.

"Oh, you alright?" I ask, while also standing.

Tony tries speaking, but can't get out words.

Someone else notices him. "Hey man, you okay?"

Tony shrugs the man off. "I'm fine!"

I put my arm around Tony.

"Let me help you." His body tightens at my touch—but he let's me help him. I feel eyes on us as we make our way out the bar; I don;t make eye contact with anyone.

"Come on big guy. This way. Let's take a little walk." Tony tries to protest, again he can't get any words out, nor does he stop allowing me to lead him.

We walk around the back of the bar, down a few steps and are now standing facing the Buffalo Bayou. I walk us a little bit further away from the bar.

What are we doing here, Madison? What's the plan?

I didn't have a plan beyond meeting Tony at the bar, getting him drunk, and maybe...I don't know trying to talk him into leaving Layla alone. After walking about 10 minutes, Tony starts regaining enough strength to push me off him.

"What the fuck? What are you doing? Who are you?" He mutters.

"You need to leave Layla alone."

"What?" He spits as he questions.

"I know what you did to those women, Tony."

"What women?"

"Layla, Jenna, Carol, Rose, Mary, all the others."

"I didn't do shit to those women!"

He loses his footing and stumbles toward the bayou.

"You know exactly what you did to those women." I seethe, jaw clenched, rage climbs up through my spine, hot and unforgiving.

"Just leave Layla alone." I take a step closer to him.

"No. I won't leave her or anyone else alone. I could have my way with you, if I wanted. But I wouldn't touch your nasty, dusty vagina even if you paid me."

I put my hands on his chest, he tries grabbing me, before he can get a hold, I shove him as hard as I can. Tony falls the short distance into the water. I hold my breath until I hear a splash. Then there is silence, no screaming, no gasping for air, no fighting for his life. Tony is gone.

The sky opens up—right on cue—with a sudden, violent release. I don't have time to think, I run back up the stairs, into the parking lot, and into my car. Slamming the door harder than I intended to, I gasp for a breath that doesn't fill me up.

Shit, shit, shit. Madison, what have you done? Did that really just happen? Did I just do that? What now?

A dark, figure passes next to my car door—I jump, *Tony?* The person keeps walking, unlocking a vehicle in the distance.

Calm down, it's just a stranger that came out of the bar. *Did he see what I did? Did he see me running up the stairs? Did anyone see me?*

I sweep my gaze across the empty parking lot, darkness pooling in every direction. The emptiness stares back, not answering a single one of my questions. My hand trembles as I press the start button on the car. The engine starts with a slow murmur. My head falls to headrest, air finally filling my lungs properly.

I didn't plan for this to happen. It just happened. However, I did suggest an obscure bar in Houston and I lured him here under false pretenses. When I arrived at the bar, I did notice the stairs that lead to the bayou right off the back of the bar—*why were you paying attention to that, Madison?* And, then, I took him down there, for what exactly? The answer not important now.

It was self-defense anyway, I tell myself as I pull out of the parking lot. I did it. I took care of Layla's problem. Now, no other woman has to be a victim of that vile man.

Detective Oliver

Joe asked for an update by the end of the day. However, I have no real update to give him. I pulled up a document half an hour ago, the blinking cursor has been staring, judging, daring me to type.

"Detective Oliver." I answer my phone on the first vibrate.

"Detective, this is Teddy. I'm down at the bayou. You had us out here searching."

"Yes?"

"We found something. You need to get down here now."

"What is it, Teddy?"

"It's a body, ma'am."

"Oh." I gasp. "Send me exactly where you are." My phone vibrates in my ear, as he has sent his location. "We'll be there in 15." I hang up and nearly run to Liam's desk.

"Woah. Normally I'm the one running into your office." Liam laughs at himself.

"We got to go!" I snap.

"Where? Why?"

"The bayou. They found another body."

"You got to be kidding me." Liam says as he grabs his stuff, following me out the door.

Liam speeds down the streets of Houston, weaving in and out of traffic, getting frustrated when cars don't move out of our way. We make it to the bayou in 10 minutes. The search crew was about a mile away from The Wild Hare bar.

"I'm Detective Oliver and this is Detective Callahan." I introduce us to the first officer we see.

"Teddy!" The officer doesn't introduce himself to us, he just calls and waves over another officer.

"I'm Teddy." The officer that walked over shakes our hands and I reintroduce us.

"Officer. Nice to meet you. Can you show us what you've found?"

"It's just Teddy, ma'am." I nod and he leads us close to the water.

Laying next to the bayou is a body-shaped figure covered with a tarp.

"M.E. asked us to keep him covered while she gets here." Teddy says. "But I'm sure she won't mind." He bends down, uncovering the body.

Liam holds his breath. A water logged, white male body lays before us. This body looks like it hasn't been in the water as long as the other ones. I could be wrong though, Ashley will let us know what she determines.

As if summoned by my thoughts, Ashley jogs over to us.

"Teddy! I told you to keep him covered!" She is clearly teasing him; I wonder if they have worked cases before.

"Sorry, Ashley." Liam coughs.

"I was only joking. I just didn't want him to cook in this sun. Boy it's getting hot already. Summer is going to be brutal." Ashley says as she puts on gloves.

When I have been on scene with a medical examiner, it has been at actual crime scenes—not with a body pulled from the water; normally, we find them in the location they die. I watch as she starts poking at the man.

"Teddy, did you find anything on the body? A driver's license? Phone?" I turn to Teddy, while Ashley does her thing.

"Yes, Damon has his wallet, keys, and chapstick that we found in his front pocket." Teddy responds, pointing to a tall, black officer packing some stuff in the back of his cruiser.

"Thank you, Teddy." I turn to Liam. "Can you and Teddy go over exactly where the body was pulled out of the water and anything else they found? I'm going to go grab his personal effects."

Liam nods and they start discussing the events of this morning that lead to pulling this person out of the bayou.

"Damon? I'm Detective Oliver." I introduce myself, hand outstretched—Damon takes my hand, shaking it, holding it just a beat too long.

"Nice to meet you. Your reputation proceeds you Detective." I almost blush.

Two months into my career as a detective, I was put on a triple homicide. Three family members were brutally beaten in their own homes, respectively. Besides being related, they didn't seem to have much in common. All other family members were cleared from any involvement in the murders. We hit a very literal dead end.

The more seasoned detectives on the case gave up—they moved onto crimes they could solve easily. This one wouldn't let me go, though. It is the only other case that kept me up at night.

After a few more months of investigations, I connected all three to one woman. All three of the deceased had a strange, tangled relationship with her. A few nights before the murders, everything blew up, resulting in the woman stabbing and torturing each family member.

The woman thought she has gotten away with the murders, but once I made the connection and brought her in for questioning, she confessed everything. While she gave up all details and evidence that was left easily, she had no remorse for what she had done.

Because of my relentlessness, I started getting assigned cases that were more challenging to solve. I assume that is why they called me as soon as a body was found in the bayou.

"I just wanted to collect the personal effects." I say to Damon.

"I was told to take it to the evidence locker."

"I understand. And that is standard protocol. However, this might be related to our other two bodies. I'll just take it from here."

He hesitates. "Is it okay if I verify with my supervisor first?"

"Of course."

I watch as he walks away to call someone, his supervisor, I assume. I pick up the bagged evidence. Keys to a Nissan, chapstick, and a wallet, just as Teddy stated. The wallet is opened in the bag, his license visible.

Christopher Grant Lawson, a 36 year-old, white male living in Houston but originally from Albuquerque, New Mexico. His criminal records in both states and in Oklahoma is about as long as Tomas's and Tony's combined. There's so much here from driving under the influence, to domestic violence, to assaulting a police officer. I really don't understand how he has gotten away with these kinds of crimes and able to walk the streets a free man.

I search for living relatives and find a sister in New Mexico, who happens to be married to a police officer. I cross reference the report with the officer he was accused of assaulting to ensure it wasn't just his brother-in-law he attacked. But no, it was a different officer, however, I assume his connection to a law enforcement officer is the reason he was not in prison for the offense.

Family member's tend to think they can get away with awful crimes just because they know someone in law enforcement. My family knows, I'd be the first one to arrest them—I am not calling in favors, jeopardizing my career and reputation because they did something illegal. However, no one in my family would commit any crimes.

"Hi, may I speak with Christine Lawson?" Honestly, I'm surprised someone answered my unexpected phone call.

"This is her," Christopher's mother says.

"I'm Detective Oliver with the Houston Police Department." The phone went dead—Christine hung up on me. I immediately call her again and the call was sent directly to voicemail.

Well that was strange. I shrug the interaction off and move through the reports sent over from the team that was investigating the bayou. Joe ensured they were able to file it quickly. They didn't find any evidence by the bayou—I'm not sure what we expected to find. No trash, no footprints, nothing linked to the three men found in the bayou in the last month.

These men were at a bar drinking and then ended up in the water. Liam knocks on my door, bringing me out of my thoughts.

"Was Chris as The Wilde Hare too?" I ask.

"Yes. How did you know?" He sits in the chair across my desk.

I shrug. "I knew you would check to see if he had the same connections with the other two."

"It looks like it. And it looks like the bar was definitely the last place each men were. I checked with Harry and the bar has a tow truck that comes by a few hours after closing and tows any cars left behind. All three vehicles are at the same impound lot. And none of them have received calls about them or anyone coming to pick them up."

"We need to search those cars." I say.

"Aida is typing up search warrants as we speak."

"Good. Hmm." I sit back in my chair. "So three men went for a drink, or two at The Wilde Hare and then ended up dead in the bayou."

"Looks that way. Harry is pulling the footage from the night Christopher was there. Imagine he also walked out of the bar with the same woman."

We let that sit between us for a moment. Two might be a coincidence, three might be something more sinister.

"We need to figure out who the woman is. Have we had any luck locating any women these men communicated with on the app?"

Liam shakes his head. "It's more challenging because the text messages inviting them to the bar were sent through a secure messaging application. We can't just pull the messages from the phone company and these other companies are not so quick to give up information."

"Yea." I nod my head. "That's the point of them. Whoever this woman is, or women, is smart."

Most likely trying to protect them self from meeting a stranger off the internet or ensuring their identity won't be found out—by the man or us.

"Hmm." I start wondering out loud, but stop—going back to my computer, pulling Christopher's phone records up on the screen. I start clicking around.

"What's up?" Liam asks. "What are you thinking?"

"Yup. That's interesting." I say pointing at the screen. "Christopher was also on the same dating application." I open up the messaging system on the dating application.

Christopher, or Chris, according to his dating profile, has dozens of conversations with women. I click on a random message.

Message to Lisa:

Good morning Beautiful!

No response from Lisa.

Message to Joanna:

Hello! Love the red hair. Your profile caught my attention, would love to connect.

Thanks! Yes, let's connect.

Christopher never responded.

Message to Brianna:

Hi gorgeous. Let me take you out sometime.

Hey handsome! I'd love to let you take me out sometime. Tell me a bit about yourself.

Great! Let's make plans. I'm new to Houston, work in IT, MMA fighter but lover at heart, love traveling and exploring new areas.

How long have you been in Houston?

Their conversation goes on with some small talk for a few more messages before Brianna asks for Chris's number—good for her taking that initiative and not waiting on him to do so. I click back over the Chris's text messages.

"Look!" Liam says. "His last text message was to a Brianna. Buttttttt," he exaggerates the word. "That's the secure number we are having trouble getting information from."

"Of course it is. Let's get Joe involved to put pressure on this company to release information to us. We have to figure out who Brianna is. And the other women." Their names are escaping me at the moment—is this pregnancy brain I've read about? Is it starting already?

THE WALK TO ASHLEY'S medical examiner's office is shorter than one would expect, so dead bodies are closer everyday. Liam joined me this time—he hates this part of the job.

"Why did you get into law enforcement if you couldn't handle dead bodies?" I ask, for about the millionth time since I met him.

"Well, obviously the uniform."

We laugh. I know people find the uniform sexy and honestly, I just don't get it. It's not sexy to wear at all. I'm thankful James never had an affinity for it. It's rather uncomfortable, at least for me, as a woman—like most things, it was made for men.

"What's so funny?" Ashley meets us in the hallway.

"Oh nothing." I roll my eyes at Liam. "Have you had any time with the latest body?"

Ashley lets out a tired breath—I don't mean to leave her out, I just don't think our silly conversation was worth repeating.

"My team has done some preliminary assessments." She leads us over to a table where a body is covered.

Liam looks like he is going to get sick.

"Are you okay?" Ashley asks. "What's with you guys getting sick in here? Y'all signed up for work that deals with dead people."

I haven't told anyone at work about the pregnancy or about getting sick at work. Liam raised his eyebrow, looking in my direction, but he doesn't speak. Neither of us answer Ashley's questions, assuming they are rhetorical.

"It looks like he was in the water for about three weeks." She raises his right hand. "He has a colles fracture on his right wrist here." She points to the area on his hand that was broken.

What this from the fall? Or was there a fight at the bayou before he went into the water?

Ashley puts his arm back down. "It does appear as if he died from drowning. All his organs look normal and we have sent out labs to determine if there was drugs or alcohol in his system at the time of death."

"He was at the same bar as the other guys, so you'll probably find some alcohol." Liam says taking two giant steps back from the body.

Ashley nods. "I'll let you know what our reports say."

"Of course," I say. "Thank you so much to you and your team for getting these initial assessments done so quickly. We really appreciate it."

"Yea, no problem," Ashley says as she covers the body back up with haste, her body tight with irritation.

Liam basically runs out of the room while Ashley and I follow, more slowly. He doesn't look back, just walks straight out to the hallway and I assume back to our offices.

"Ashley," I turn to her and she looks surprised I have stopped. "Want to get coffee sometime this week?" I ask.

Her face lights up like she just unboxed a puppy on Christmas morning. "Yes! I would love to!"

Madison

I hold my breath as I refresh all the local news websites—no stories about a body found in the bayou, no missing person stories.

Ellie's contact pops up, startling me. *Deep breath, Madison.*

"Hey, Ellie."

"Hey!"

After the general pleasantries. Ellie finally says, "So Tony just left? Just like that?"

I had texted her a quick update that Tony left Layla.

I look away from the camera, knowing I cannot lie directly to Ellie. "Yea. It was the weirdest thing. She has asked him to leave and he did."

"Yea, that's really weird. I didn't expect a man like that to just leave." She is right, it is suspicious.

"Honestly, he probably had another woman on the hook and just went to her." Tony seemed to bed hop from woman to woman, so it's believable.

"Doesn't that scare you too? That he could be out there doing the same to another woman right now?"

"You're the one who told me I can only worry about getting him away from Layla right now."

"You're right." She sighs. "Did she end up going to the police or getting the restraining order?"

I sigh too. She knows the answer—women don't get to go to the authorities because they fear retaliation or fear they won't be helped.

"I am so afraid for my daughter to date one day."

We sit in silence for what feels like forever.

"Oh, did you get your test results back from the doc-tor?"

"Yea, everything's fine." I almost choke on my hard swal-low.

"Kevin..."

"Work," I don't let her get her question out. "Actually, I should go. I'll probably call Layla again and make sure she is okay and hasn't heard from Tony."

"Okay, bye, love you, Madison." She isn't satisfied with how this conversation went, I can tell. I've know Ellie long enough to understand this and she has known me long enough to know there's more I am not saying.

"Love you too, Ellie." I hang up before tears come.

Still no news updates on a body found or a missing person.

What if they find him? What if they link it to me? That's impossible. Well, nothing is impossible, or so they say. *However, they haven't linked the first one to you, so maybe they won't ever; not then, not now, not in the future.*

I open up the dating application logged into Clare's profile.

Should I still be doing this? Do I even think I can find a decent man for someone else? Maybe I should just quietly bow out, now. My thoughts are interrupted by notifications.

Message from Mark:

> What would the book be about? I'd read it no matter what. Mine would have to be starting my own business. I've always wanted to be my own boss.

Wait, Mark, I thought your profile said you were 'self-employed'? I ponder a moment before responding, but I don't go back to his profile.

> That book would probably be a kids book or young adult novel, but not exactly sure. Own your own business, that's a good goal as well. What would you do?

> Not one hundred perfect sure, either. That's why I haven't done it yet. But probably something with AI - it's so hot right now. Speaking of, you aren't some bot are you?

> Nope, I'm a real girl. Maybe we can exchange numbers to tell for sure.

I click over to the conversation with Jonathan.

Message from Jonathan:

> There really isn't a great place around here to hike, being Houston and all. I do like some of the trails. Might not be the safest place to meet a stranger. We could do coffee instead, some-where in public and well-lit.

Both men were very responsive—must have been on the application messaging women back or scrolling for more likes. I give Jonathan the phone number I created for Clare. He texted from his number right away. I just hope his isn't a fake one as well. Mark also gives me his number. Armed with phone numbers, photos, and names, I begin my research. This time, I won't be fooled.

First up, Jonathan. I post his picture and name in the Facebook group. While I wait for replies, I enter his phone number into the identity verification website I now pay for. His full name pops up immediately, along with other possible phone number and addresses. Clicking back over to Facebook, I type in his full name and find his profile—the same pictures are on this site as the dating site. So far, all the information on this site is the same as on the other. I take a deep breath, realizing I had been holding it all along.

Next, I type Jonathan's name into Google, a few other social media accounts are found, however these are completely private. A preview of his LinkedIn comes up showing his latest place of employment. This job seems to match the one listed on his dating profile. I type the hospital he is employed at into Google and search through employees. Jonathan's picture comes up with a small bio of his medical background.

Circling back to Facebook, I check my post—which has gotten a few comments.

Comments:

Dede: Jonathan! He's such a good guy!

Marie: I work with this man. He's actually a really good guy!

Jamie: I talked to him briefly months ago. He's ready for way more than I was at the time. But he was respectable, funny man and we had a great time together.

Sage: This is my ex. What these women are saying is true. He is an amazing guy. We only broke up because my career took me elsewhere.

I am surprised and happy by what I am reading, but still skeptical. They always seem too good to be true.

Mark's turn. I perform all of the same steps for him that I did for Jonathan. The name that comes up under his phone number is T Mark; does that mean his first name isn't Mark?

This time on the identification website 'potential criminal charges' is highlighted. This means he has something on his record. I click the link, the site prompts my to pay an extra $2.50 to read the report. I don't need to pay; I could search county records but this report will same me the trouble of searching each county site—so I pay the fee and download the report.

While I wait, I click back to the Facebook post; 138 comments. *Oh shit*, I hold my breath.

Comments:

Emma: I don't think Mark is his first name. It's possible it's his last. Talked to him a few months ago. Came on aggressive, basically moved into my house the first night. I asked him to pay for something and he bounced. Never seen or heard from him again.

Jennifer: Did someone say his ex stabbed him?

Kimberly: Repeat offender, search his name.

Angela: We matched a couple of different apps. But he always disappeared/unmatched. I matched with him again just to ask why he keeps matching and disappearing. His response...he disappeared again. The last time we matched he apologized and said he wanted to get to know me. I have

a big Instagram account and one my videos popped up on his feed. He followed me and send me his IG. We had great conversation and everything good. The next day I realized he has blocked me and unmatched again.
Rachel: Goes by his last name on these apps now. I think he got banned with his real name. He is smart and charming and really funny but is actually a super spreader monster criminal with no morals or values. Claims to have his own solar panel business, but really just a narcissistic fraud/scammer with an extensive criminal record but you wouldn't be able to tell by how he presents himself. I was good friends with this man for 10 years, so he'll also play the long game! I contacted his ex before me and sure enough he pulled the same gaslighting manipulative narcissist serial cheater sad story shit to her too. He caught 2 new felonies within the last month.
Elizabeth: Please DM me; especially if you have met in person.

While reading the comments, the criminal record has downloaded—I pause and hover the cursor over the file. I don't know if I'm prepared for what this report contains, not after these comments. The report is pages long, I only thought I was getting a headache reading the comments. Domestic violence, criminal trespassing, aggravated assault;

the list, the dates, everything goes on and on. How is this man walking free?

I click back over to Facebook and message Elizabeth asking about Mark. She responds immediately.

A lot of comments already addressed his name and other things. Long story long. We met in AZ a few years ago and then he moved to TX. We continued to do the long distance thing until I caught him cheating. I ended it but we remained friends. I moved to TX and we got close again. He asked if we could give it another shot….when he was in prison again. The man sold the dream, he was my best friend and nobody could tell me anything about this man. I stupidly supported him. I should have made him leave, but we were in love. After 2 months, I found out I was pregnant. Instead of being excited, he got extremely angry. We got into a very heated argument in which he 1. claimed the baby couldn't be his, 2. denied I was even pregnant, 3. threatened to call his lawyers to "bury" me, 4. and maybe I should have lead with this, he pulled a knife on me. I wrestled it from him and actually stabbed him in the leg. We called 911 and he was arrested. I lost the baby, of course he didn't care. I had to get a restraining order against him and call the police multiple times when he violated it. I had thought he was in prison again, but I guess he is out on the streets. Stay away, stay very far away.

Tears form in the corners of my eyes, they sting. Then I see red. The same darkness clouds my vision, just like it did years ago in my childhood bedroom.

Detective Oliver

Does Houston have three coincidental accidents or a serial killer?

We do have three dead men. Each man was on a dating application. Each man had a conversation with a woman that invited him out. Each man went to the same bar. Each man ended up in the bayou, drowned. Each man had alcohol in his system and potentially drugs (the tests were unfortunately inconclusive).

Here's what we know about each—and what I run through in my head, every day and every night.

Tony Aaron Jones, 31, Houston native, unemployed and essentially homeless. No apparent family besides sister, Britt, whom accused Tony of raping her and seemed relieved he is dead. Lengthy criminal record, in which he should have been in prison along time for. Tony was on a dating application. The last place he was seen at was The Wilde Hare. He last texted a Layla. Tony walked out of the bar with an unknown woman and was the first body to go into the Buffalo Bayou, drowning. There was alcohol and maybe drugs in his system.

Tomas Elian Mark, 27, Colorado native, self-employed and living in small studio apartment in the city. His parents have been divorced for many years—neither have heard from Tomas in months prior to his death. Tomas also had a similar and lengthy criminal record as Tony did. He was also on the same dating application. Finally, the last place Tomas was seen was The Wilde Hare. His last text message, inviting him to the bar, was from a Clare. Tomas, too stumbled out of the bar with a similar unknown woman. Tomas's body was found in the bayou first, however, he went in the water after Tony. There was alcohol and possibly drugs in his system.

Christopher Grant Lawson, 36, New Mexico native, IT specialist and lived in an apartment alone just outside the city. We only have his mother's information, however, we have not been able to connect with her. Chris's criminal record is just as long as the other two men's records, he was on the dating application, and last known location was The Wilde Hare. The woman who asked Chris to meet him was a Brianna. After reviewing footage from the bar, Chris also left the bar with our unknown female. His wrist broke, either before or on the way into the bayou and he drown as well.

Liam feels like these are enough similar attributes to connect the cases. While I agree, all three cases are eerily similar, we need more evidence to make any real conclusions.

The first thing we need to do is locate these women. Tony's phone records had two numbers for Layla—one from the secure messaging application and one from the regular phone messaging application. We have yet to receive any information from either as to who is behind the numbers; if it's a female named Layla or someone else entirely.

I sit across from Ashley at the coffee shop a few blocks from the station—my go to for a quick hit of caffeine mid-day.

"Is caffeine okay while pregnant?" Ashley asks; I roll my eyes. "Oh, sorry. Or are you not pregnant?" She covers her face for assuming again.

I nod. "Oh I am. And you sound just like James."

He keeps telling me I need to cut the caffeine for the baby; I considered it, but I consulted the internet, so for now, I'll keep enjoying my coffee. I smile and then it's quickly wiped from my face, as anxiety sets in.

"What's wrong?"

I shake my head. "Google says two cups is okay." I say, putting my coffee cup up to my lips, but not drinking it. "Please don't tell anyone at work. I'm not ready to tell anyone yet."

"I understand." She says.

"How have you liked being a medical examiner?" I ask, changing the subject.

"I really cannot believe how much I love it!"

"Can you tell me what excites you about cutting up bodies all day?"

She laughs. "Well, that's one way of putting it. But it's not about cutting up the bodies." She pauses to gather her thoughts. "Okay, maybe it's a little bit about cutting up bodies."

We both laugh.

"Tell me what more there is to it?" I take small sips of my coffee, savoring the hot liquid.

"It's a puzzle. Especially at the examiner's office. Before I was just dressing the dead for their loved ones. Which I liked doing, but they came to us when everything was said and done and the family was ready to put the person in the ground. I like being in this in-between space. I get to help families understand what happened to their loved ones between death and burying them."

I nod along, because I actually understand. The search for truth, to understand, to be able to give answers is intoxicating. I got into law enforcement to help people, to be someone I needed when I was younger.

"I understand that." I finally tell her.

"Yea, I mean, I figured you did." She pauses. "I still can't believe we ended up at the same place. I knew you were an officer, thanks to our moms on Facebook, but I didn't know where. I also wasn't sure where I would exactly end up."

I give a 'ha-ha.' "Yea, small world."

She places her hand on my hand and I try not to pull back quickly.

"I'm really sorry about what happened between us all those years ago," she says.

The past hangs thick in the air between us. I suck in, trying to take a breath before it escapes me.

"I had no idea. I wish you had told me." She says.

"I tried." I say in a whisper.

"I know. I can see that now. I didn't understand any thing that was going on back then." She takes her hand back and looks down at the table.

I spent too many years being angry at everyone involved. I forgave Ashley a long time ago, but when I saw she was the new medical examiner, it took me back to that night almost 20 years ago.

"Where's Ashley?" I asked Brad, star quarterback and Ashley's boyfriend.

He handed me a red cup filled with a mixture of alcohols and juices—basically whatever Brad's dad had in the fridge. Brad was being raised by his father only; his mom ran off when he was about two. Brad's dad was a retired, powerful attorney, had a lot of money, and was always jetsetting around the world, leaving Brad and his brother Brandon home alone. So every other weekend, we were at their house, partying like any teenager would do.

"She passed out in my room hours ago." He shrugged it off, sitting next to me on the couch. We were the last ones awake, friends passed out all around us.

"Oh man, I thought she might be awake still." I downed the contents of the cup in two gulps.

Brad touched my empty cup to his full one. "That right, champ."

We sat next to each other in silence for ten minutes before I got up to use the bathroom. The room spun as soon as I stood. I made it to the bathroom, but when I got out my world went dark and my memories of the rest of the night are spotty.

Brad was waiting for me to get out of the bathroom. I asked to go to bed and he led me to the guest room I normally slept in. I thought I went in alone, but my next memory was of Brad on top of me. I know I tried pushing him off of me. The next memory I have, Brad was still on top of me, but this time we didn't have clothes on. I screamed, or at least I tried. I woke up the next day, covered in blood, sweat, and shame.

I knew what to do though, I didn't go shower, I didn't even go home. I went straight to the hospital. I told the nurse what happened—I thought she believed me. They gave me an IV and called my parents. I asked for a rape kit and they did one, but also questioned how much I had to drink. The officer called to take my statement knew Brad's dad and put away his notebook as soon as he heard it was at his house.

I asked the doctor to test my blood for drugs—my parents horrified I would do drugs.

"I didn't do drugs!" I nearly screamed. "I *was* drugged."

"Honey," my mom did her best to comfort me, while also discrediting me. "I think you just had too much to drink."

I didn't just have too much to drink and I knew it. I remember everything before the drink Brad handed me—and it wasn't much. I had drank more and not felt this way the next day. I had drank more and remembered what happened to me.

My parents grounded me for partying, even though they knew where I was and what we were doing before hand, but grounding a teenager officially getting caught drinking sounded like the right parenting choice. The rape kit was lost and the police report was never filed. I was just another girl who cried rape. Just another statistic.

Madison

"Where were you?" Robbie hands me a coffee.

"You brought me a coffee?" I take a sip, he even got it with my typical milk alternative. "I just had a lot going on. Took a few days to regroup."

"I need your help!" Robbie whines.

"So, that's why you brought me a coffee with soy milk?" The bribery, which is so Robbie, tastes like dark roast bitterness softened with cream, familiar and effective.

"No," he blushes. "Well, kind of."

I roll my eyes. "I need to get some of this work done. My inbox was flooded this morning." I turn back to my computer, telling him to leave me alone now, he gets the hint and goes to Lauri's cubicle. I ignore their conversation, but I'm not exactly working.

My inbox is flooded with emails, like the bayou flooded two days ago after a spontaneous storm that rolled through the city. I anxiously awaited Tony's body to pop up.

Text to Mark:

Hey Mark, it's Clare!

Hey Clare! I am happy to hear from you. How are you today?

I am surprised at his quick response, however, I am glad it's quick—this should be easy.

I'm great! Just working. How are you?

I am great as well. Just working too. When can I take you out?

I am free Sunday evening.

Perfect. We'll plan something *kissy face emoji*

Easy as pie. I cannot imagine the hell he would have put Clare through if I had actually set them up—it makes me sick, actually.

I pull up the Houston news site on my computer. There are still no reports of a body found or a missing person report. I guess no one really cared for Tony; not surprising.

Beep. Beep. Beep.

"Hey guys! Just wanted to check in again. I am still reading all your wonderful comments and messages. I've started organizing requests, it's a lot to get through. I am still working with a second client. You guys weren't kidding when you said it's difficult finding good men in this city! I've learned a lot and got a more robust vetting system. Thanks for all the support!" #ghostdater

I blow a kiss to the camera and post the video.

I finally gave Clare Jonathan's information. We had a little bit more conversation and with the raving reviews and clean record, I feel a little comfortable allowing her to go out with him. I did advise her to take it slow and maybe have at least one video call before meeting him a well-lit public place.

Maybe instead of setting women up with men, I need to teach them safe practices while dating men. I guess I will have to do both.

Text from Mark:

> Looking forward to seeing you
> tonight *kissy face emoji*

Me too! See you soon!

I spot Mark sitting alone at the bar. Unlike Tony, he picked a seat that faces the door. I take the empty seat to his right, leaving the other one on his left. An empty glass sits in front of him.

"Welcome in, ma'am." A bartender sets a napkin in front of me—thankfully, it's a different bartender.

"Thanks, I'll take a spicy margarita." Before I could re-think ordering the same drink as the night I was here with Tony, he turns to make the drink.

"Good choice." I'm surprised Mark acknowledges me.

"I'll have one too," he yells to the bartender.

"Is that what you were drinking?" I nod to his glass.

"Yea." He moves to stand. "I am going to run to the restroom, make sure no one takes my drink." He winks.

He's still gone when our drinks arrive. I put my hand on the top of both glasses, pulling them closer, dropping drugs in Mark's glass—it disappears without making a sound, a bubble, or a ripple.

"Thank you."

Mark startles me. "Oh," I say as my heart beats in my ears. "No problem. I made sure no one slipped you anything." We laugh.

I hold up my glass to his. "Cheers." We say in unison.

I only take a small sip of mine. Again, surprisingly, Mark makes small talk with me while periodically checking his phone.

"Waiting on someone?" I finally ask.

"Yea, a first date. Guess she stood me up."

"Bummer."

"It happens." He shrugs. He doesn't seem angry that he's been stood up and presumably ghosted. He asks why I haven't touched my drink.

"Oh, I've just been enjoying our conversation so much." I take another small sip while he orders himself another drink. He closes out his tab and pays for my drink as well. Now, I understand why women fall for this man; he is charming. We keep chatting while he finishes his drink.

"You know, Ashley, you aren't normally my type. But I've enjoyed talking to you." At some point, I told him my name is Ashley.

"Um, well I don't know exactly how to take that, Tomas."

"What?" He introduced himself as Mark, of course. I thought in person, he would at least use his real first name, but he didn't.

"How?" He asks.

I just smile at him.

"You know what, you fat bitch." He stands, wobbling on his feet.

"Woah, bud. You okay there?" I taunt him just a little.

The alcohol, the drugs hit him and he can't speak. I stand to help him walk out to the bar, just as I had done with Tony. Again, I lead him down to the bayou and away from the bar. I keep my eyes on the water, expecting Tony to pop up any moment.

After a few minutes of walking, I stop to take a breath. Mark manages to push me away, but his legs won't support his weight, he falls.

"What the fuck did you do to me?"

"Nothing you haven't done to lots of women, Tomas Mark."

"Fuck you." He looks helplessly up at me.

"April, Anika, Vanessa, Alice, Gra…"

"What are you doing?" He cuts me off.

"Let me finish. Grace, Sofia, Evelyn, Mia, Olivia, Rachel, Liz, Naomi, Cora. I know what you did the each of them."

"How could you? Who are you?" At least, that is what I think he says.

"Don't worry about that."

I can tell he's getting more light-headed; his world is probably spinning by now. He is no longer sitting up—looking more pathetic lying on the ground. *It's time, Madison.* I roll his body closer to the drop off; this proves more difficult than I expected. Mark is heaver than Tony, and Tony was on his feet, stumbling to his death.

"What are you..." Mark tries to get out as I push his legs over the bayou wall.

One more shove and the rest of his body goes over the edge. The splash of the water is deafening. Just like Tony, because of the drugs and the alcohol, there's no struggle. He lets the water take him down. I stare into the darkness for a moment more.

Detective Oliver

I don't blame Ashley for anything—she didn't do anything really. But that was the problem, no one did anything. I lost a lot that night, most of my friends—including Ashley—and a lot of myself and my way for a little bit. Eventually, the injustice in what happened to me lead me to trying to get justice for others. Honestly, I don't think I'd be here without that night, but I also wish I didn't have to go through all of it either.

My phone rings, jolting me out my thoughts—it's been an hour since Ashley and I had coffee. She gave me a heartfelt apology and told me how glad she was that we get a second chance at friendship. I told her I'd like that, but it is going to take some time.

"Detective Oliver." I answer the phone.

"Christine here. You called the other day." The woman on the other end introduces herself.

"Yes. Thank you for calling..." Christine starts talking before I can finish my sentence.

"If this has anything to do with Chris, I haven't seen him in years. Or talked to him in ages. Oh gosh, I can't even remember our last conversation."

"Ma'am. I hate to tell you this over the phone," she interrupts before I can finish, again.

"I saw you sent local police to my house. We weren't home."

"Yes, I understand. I am with the Houston Police Department, as I stated in my message. Chris has been living in Houston for a few months." I pause, waiting on her to say something—she doesn't. "Chris was found a few days ago in the bayou, deceased."

"Oh." She gasps. "Really? Are you sure it's my son Chris?"

"Yes, ma'am. DNA tests confirmed."

"Well. Damn."

"His death is a part of an ongoing investigation."

"Investigation? Why?"

"We have reason to believe his death might not have been an accident."

"Oh. Hm. Well, like I said, I haven't seen or spoken to him in years."

The coldness. All three of these men's families have had this coldness to the news that their family member has died. It's...interesting. If I got a call my brother had passed and maybe it was intentional, I would be devastated and do all I could to help the investigation and catch who did it. Then again, my brother doesn't have a criminal past like these men do.

I ask her a few more questions about Chris's past and his potential whereabouts. She doesn't tell me anything I didn't find out through his criminal and phone records. She also would like us to cremate his body and do away with the ashes when the investigation is over. She requested I not contact her again.

Liam appeared at my door right as I am hanging up with Christine. I shake my head.

"What's up?" He asks.

"These families are so heartless." I say.

"It makes sense now why no one has made any missing person reports." I nod; he's right. It also makes sense why these men committed horrible crimes—individuals exposed to childhood maltreatment or abuse are 50% more likely to commit crimes as an adult.

I tell Liam about the call with Christine.

"You believe she hasn't seen him?"

"I do. We'll need to call the rest of his family. He has a brother-in-law in law enforcement."

"Ready?" Liam finally gets back to the reason he came into my office. I get my stuff without answering him—we got a search warrant easily for Chris's apartment and found his keys in his car in the impound lot the tow truck took it from the bar.

We both look down at our phones that beeped at the same time. An email from Harry, the bar owner, containing footage of Chris. Liam and I pause, open the email clicking on the video.

"Is that the same woman?" Liam asks.

"Looks really similar. Why is it just her back again?"

We continue walking.

"Hey Aida," Liam says as we are waking by her desk. "I'm forwarding you this footage from the bar. Can you compare the woman with Chris to the footage of Tony and Tomas?"

"Of course." Aida says, happily.

"Houston Police Department." Liam yells into Chris's apartment. He walks the premise ahead of me to ensure no one was in the space. As we expected, it was clear.

Chris lives in a nice apartment complex in an area of Houston called the Heights. His third floor, one bedroom apartment is only a little more than 600 square feet, according to the complex's website. While the place is nice and in a decent area of town, his unit is bare. We know he moved to Houston a few months ago, but there's no couch, no TV, not even a bed—just a mattress on the floor.

"How is a man who is living like this, on a dating app?" I ask Liam.

"I looked through the rest of his messages on the app and texts, he wasn't doing very well on there."

"Makes sense." We walked in five minutes ago and have made it through the whole place. There is the mattress on the floor, a toothbrush, one towel, and that's it—no dishes, no trash, not even a blanket on the mattress.

"Maybe he spent all his money on the deposit?"

"Have you talked to his employer?" I ask. Chris worked as an IT specialist for a company headquartered in Florida.

"Yea. They said he has disappeared for a few weeks at a time, sometimes. They were just gathering more evidence to be able to fire him."

I shake my head, I think even with the Police Officers Union on my side, I'd still get fired for not showing up to work every day. *Why did this man keep getting a pass from society?*

I'm unboxing a white cake when James gets home. He drops the bags of food and immediately hugs me from behind, rubbing my belly that's starting to protrude. James texted me asking what my latest pregnancy craving is—he wants to make tonight special. My latest craving, though, is sushi. Unfortunately, raw fish is not good for the baby and that is one rule, I will stick to. So I had to go with the next thing, steak and deep fried potatoes. Starchy carbs have been my go to since I've been pregnant. It should have been my first sign, since they aren't something in my normal diet.

"That just looks delicious." James says pointing to the cake. "What if," he turns me around to face him. "What if we cut into that first?" His eyes light up at the thought of having cake before dinner.

"How could I say no to that?" He almost jumps up and down. I get the knife and some plates while he puts the food in the oven to stay warm.

"How does this work? Should we record it?" James asks.

"We just cut into it. If it's pink, we are having a girl and blue, a boy." I shrug. "Yea, we probably should record it, huh?"

The manner in which people find out the gender of their baby, can take many forms and over the years, people have gone all out. My family isn't too happy that I have opted for a quiet cake cutting at home with just James and me. If my mom had it her way, we would invite anyone she ever met to a party at her house. She tried to do that for our wedding—we had to limit the amount of people she could invite.

I take some pictures of the cake, while James sets up a tripod with his phone. I have never been good at documenting our life, but I know we should start being more intentional with it, especially for the baby to have later. If I actually watch a crime documentary, I see all the videos and photos they have of the victim—I wonder what my parents would be able to provide if something were to happen to me like that; I know for a fact we have zero videos of me as a child. Well that's morbid, I'm not just taking videos and photos in case something tragic happens to my child later on in life.

"It's ready to go," James says and we gather next to each other in front of the phone.

I pick up the knife saying, "Let's do this together."

He places his hand over mine; we make a small cut in the cake, pulling it up together to make another cut.

"It's pink," I whisper.

"Huh?" James didn't notice the frosting on the knife when we pulled it out of the first cut. "Oh! It's a girl!"

"It's a girl!" I have tears in my eyes. I am so excited to be having a baby, I honestly didn't really care either way—I know people always say that, but we wanted this so badly—I mean it.

Together, we finish cutting the cake and serve ourselves each a piece of white cake with pink filling. Before we eat, we embrace, taking a deep breath together.

We are having a baby girl.

I'm still nervous about telling people we are pregnant, but I put a quick meeting on Liam and Joe's schedules to let them know first—one being my partner and one being my boss.

Liam knocks on my door in the middle of a yawn. "Hey, I know we have a meeting set later today." He pauses.

"Oh man, Liam. You look tired."

"Got called in again in the middle of the night."

"I thought Joe told them to take you off being on call?"

He shrugs and yawns again, showing me every single one of his teeth. "He did, but the detective on call was sick or something."

"Gotcha. What's up Liam?"

"They found a body in the Brays Bayou."

"Okay? When?"

"About an hour before you got in. They want us on it, may be connected?"

"Hmm. May...be. I guess all bodies found in a bayou is ours now?"

He shrugs and we head out to the scene.

Madison

"Madison! I called you so many times!" Ellie screams through the phone.

Now, I wish I hadn't called her back.

"I know, I'm sorry."

"Are you going to tell me where you have been?"

"Kev and I went out most of the weekend. I left my phone at the apartment," I lie.

"You can't do that!"

"Okay, Ellie," I snap.

"Sorry, I am just so worried about you."

"There's nothing to worry about." I sigh. Ellie took on the motherly role as soon as she found out mine had died.

"How are you feeling?"

"I've been feeling fine," I lie again.

"I called your doctor."

"I'm going to hang up on you. Ellie! You did what? Ellie, that is a total violation of my privacy. And against

HIPPA laws or something. What. The. Hell." Heat rises in my cheeks.

"It's actually not, Madison Lily. You put me down as someone who has access to your medical records, remember?" I didn't remember; however, since Ellie is the closest person to me, it make sense. It's not like I'd put my dad as my medical contact.

"It's fine. I'm fine."

"You aren't though." Ellie's eyes start watering. "Why didn't you tell me you are sick again?"

"Because it's not a big deal. It just is what it is at this point. And I'm not really sick right now. I've got no symptoms at all."

Ellie can no longer speak—she is full-on sobbing. I just listen to her until Nick takes the phone from her.

"Hey, Madison. I'll have Ellie call you back later." We hang up without another word.

I guess I understand Ellie's reaction, but also, people get sick and die every day. I always knew my time would come sooner rather than later.

BEEP. BEEP. BEEP.

"Happy Valentine's Day loves! I hope you all are enjoying your day, whether you are in a couple or single. I just heard from my second client and she is headed on a very special date! I will be reaching out to another lucky lady this evening to become my third client and hopeful she won't be alone this day next year. I am really loving being able to set up you beautiful ladies! Lots of love!" #ghostdater

I blow the camera a kiss—my signature, I guess. I upload the video before I head to a bar for a drink; since I'm dying anyway, might as well enjoy myself. I've been stressing all week waiting on Mark—er, Tomas's—body to be discovered or a missing persons report. Neither have happened yet.

My ring tone startles me; normally, my phone is on silent. I hit the green answer button before thinking.

"Hello?" My dad says as a question after I didn't say anything when I answered the call. I sigh hearing his voice.

"Hi, dad." I'm sure he can hear my eye roll through the phone.

"Madison, when are you coming home?"

"I don't know." I can't have this conversation again.

"You sound exhausted. Are you sleeping well?"

"Yes, dad." Actually, no, but he doesn't really care either way.

"You aren't sick again? Are you?"

I don't immediately answer his question. My mind flashes back to the doctor's office. I basically lived in doctor's offices—for years it was only for check ups, given the all clear to go live my life, finally. However, the last visit was different. It's never good when they want to see you in person to give you test results. These were the ones I've been expecting since the beginning.

"I can't lose you too, Madison." My dad says, bursting my thoughts.

Too late, dad. You lost me a long time ago.

"Come home so I can take care of you. I can protect you."

I nearly laugh out loud. *Protect me? Where was his protection when I really needed it?* He didn't shield me from his drunk, destructive ways. Didn't protect me from my own cousin and his monstrous ways.

"I'm fine. I can take care of myself. I got to go." I press the red end call button, without another word.

Detective Oliver

It's a steamy day outside—Ashley was right, Houston is going to have a hot summer. I am not prepared for it, nor am I looking forward to it while putting on weight growing a baby. It feels even hotter being at the bayou, filled with stagnant water. I've got to start carrying bug spray in my bag. *Is West Nile still a concern for pregnant women?*

The officers at the scene have processed what little evidence they found. The body is already on a stretcher, ready to head to the medical examiner's office. I'm surprised Ashley told them to go ahead and not wait on her to get here.

Liam walks the bayou looking around at the scene while the officer uncovers the body for me to look at. The baby is isn't making me nauseous anymore, I can finally breathe and work.

The body is water-logged, of course, but it's not as bad as some of the other ones. This could be an indication he wasn't in the water as long. I'll let Ashley tell me exactly how long he was in the water and approximate day and time of death.

"Did he have a phone or any identification on him?" I ask the officer as he covered the body back up. He motioned for another officer to load the body up to take it away. Honestly, I'm not sure why we came out here to begin with, just like Ashley, we could have waited until the body and his belongings made it down to the station.

"Actually, he did."

I'm as surprised as he is; how have we gotten lucky with the last two victims having their identification on them?

"I've got a phone, but it's probably got a lot of water damage. And there's a wallet. The license said a Matthew or something? I don't remember. I figure I leave the detective work up to you guys." He gives the man's personal effects to me and I go grab Liam.

"Find anything significant?" I ask him.

"No."

"We've got a Matthew." I hold up the evidence bags. "We've got a phone and wallet again. So, that's something."

As we start driving back to the office, Liam points out a bar along the bayou. "You think this guy was in a bar before he went in the water?"

"Might be worth it to stop in."

He turns around to drive into the parking lot of the bar. I feel like this is an area I drive by often, but never knew this place existed. Twist & Tonic Bar and Grill. It's only noon, but it's open already—they must focus on food as well to be open so early.

"Hi, I'm Detective Oliver. This is Detective Liam." I say to the worker before she can even greet us. Panic crosses her face. "Can we speak with a manager or an owner?" She relaxes—I wonder what that was about, but I don't think she has anything to do with our immediate case, as she doesn't fit the woman's description. We will question her later, though.

"Oh, uh. Yea. I'll go get him." She disappears and Liam and I start walking around the small bar. I'm taking in atmosphere, the lighting, the tables, the patrons.

"Hi officers." A tall, bearded man greets us. The girl from the front takes her position back at the door. I can feel her avoidance.

I reintroduce Liam and myself to him and he introduces himself to us—his name is Jamal and is the owner of the bar.

"How can I help you?" He leads us to an open table and we sit.

"We have an open investigation and were wondering if you could help us?" I show Jamal Matthew's driver's license—still in the evidence bag.

"I don't understand," He says.

"Do you know if this man was in this bar? Within the last few weeks?" I ask.

"Hm." He takes a closer look but doesn't touch the bag. "Actually, he does look familiar."

Liam's face lights up. "He was in here?"

"I think so, maybe a week or so ago. I mean it's hard to tell, but I have seen him a few times in here. The last time, he was with a girl. Well I don't think they came in together, but they left together."

"A girl?" I question.

"Woman. Sorry. Yea. I only really remember him because he started slurring and appeared very intoxicated. The woman helped him out."

"Did you happen to see if they got into a vehicle?"

"I didn't. They were in the parking lot for a few minutes. I assumed she took him home or called an Uber for him."

"You assumed? Are you normally in the practice of letting highly intoxicated people just stumble out and find their own way home? Even if it means they drive drunk and kill themselves or someone else?" Liam shoots me a pointed look after I make this comment.

Jamal shakes his head and sighs. "No, never. We have never had any issues with that. Since he left with someone, that's a good sign she helped him home."

"We understand." Liam puts his hand up in defense, or maybe to call a truce; we need Jamal's willing assistance, after all.

I take a deep breath. "Do you have cameras outside or in the bar?"

"We do. I can get you footage from that night. Can I take down his name so I can look up our credit card records to see when he was here?" Jamal says.

"Of course. Can you tell us anything more about the woman he left with?"

"It's going to sound awful for me to say this, but no. She was a generic white woman. I was surprised she was able to help the man outside, he was really leaning his weight on her, but she was able to get both of them out."

"What do you mean by that?" I ask.

"Generic white woman?"

I shake my head before he can expand on that.

"Oh, I just mean she looked like she might be sick or something. She was...what's the word. Frail."

I look questioning at Liam.

"Thank you Jamal. You have been very helpful. If you could get us the footage, the name of employees working that night so we can question them, and all the information on who was here that night, that would be great." Liam says and stands.

"Of course. I will go get on that. Let me know if you all need anything else." Jamal says as he also stands.

I push myself up from the table as well. We shake hands and leave the bar.

"Well, that was interesting," Liam says as we get in the car.

"Yea it was," I pause. "I'm pregnant." I blurt out.

"Is it mine?" Liam laughs at himself.

I hit his arm. "You're so stupid."

"I know. Congratulations! I'm excited for you and James. For real."

"Thanks," I start rubbing my belly, relieved someone knows and hoping nothing bad is going to happen now that someone knows.

"Hey," I say before Liam gets out of the car, back at the station. "No one knows about the pregnancy yet. Well now you know, but that's it."

"I won't tell anyone."

"Thanks."

We walk into the station, greeted by Aida.

"Do you think the new body is related too?" She asks immediately.

I shrug. "Time will tell. But he was at a bar, we think the night he went into the bayou, and left with a woman."

Aida's eyes light up—she oddly seemed to get excited about being a part of a serial killer case.

"On that note. Layla is in conference room one. She just got here."

I look at her confused.

"The woman Tony was dating." She jogs my memory and I nearly sprint to the conference room.

Layla is gorgeous, her long brown hair pulled back away from her face, her blue eyes pierce a hole straight through me. She is shaking—*because she is involved in Tony's death? —Or just because she is nervous to be in a police station?*

"Thank you for coming down here Layla." Liam joined me in the conference room with Layla. We do the normal introductions and sit. Layla is gripping a paper cup of coffee; any harder and she will put a hole in it.

"We understand you were dating a Tony Jones," Liam starts the conversation.

Layla nods.

"Can you tell us how you met?"

"Through a dating app. Is he is some kind of trouble?"

"Can you tell us the last time you saw or talked to Tony?"

"It's been a few months." She pauses to think. "About January or so."

"Was that the last time you talked to him or saw him?" Liam asks.

"Both. I asked him to leave my house. And he actually did. He never came back. Never tried contacting me."

"Was he staying the night there? Living with you?"

Layla sighs; she looks exhausted. "He was basically living with me."

"And you didn't think him leaving and not coming back or calling wasn't suspicious?" I sound a little more harsh than I intend.

She doesn't immediately answer, so Liam says, "Can you take us through your relationship with Tony?"

"We met from the dating app at the beginning of January. We hit it off and it moved way quicker than I wanted. He essentially moved in after a week or so."

Liam is trying to hold back his judgment but his face is giving it all away when I look at him—I am definitely judging his judging.

"I know. But we spent a lot of time together. There's no kids involved. He lied and told me he was having issues with his apartments, so he needed a place to stay for a little bit. It was all a lie. All of it." She puts her face in her hands.

"Take your time." Liam comforts her.

"Just as quickly as we seemed to fall in love, the abuse started."

"What abuse?" I say, trying to sound empathetically but I don't know if it comes out like that.

"All of the emotional abuse, physical. You name it. He controlled me. I couldn't leave my house. He tracked my location. He went through my phone."

"In a manner of weeks?"

She nods her head and is clearly ashamed.

"Did you report this abuse?" *Please let there be documentation*, I silently plead.

"Not to authorities. I have photos and messages." She pulls out her phone.

"You don't have to pull them up right now, but we will need all of that for our investigation." Liam tells her.

"By the end of January, I couldn't take it any more. I told him to leave. He refused, but then one day, he actually did. I was just so relieved that I didn't have to deal with all of that anymore."

"Just like that? You didn't hear from him again?"

"Nope." She shrugs the memory away.

"We understand," Liam says, looking to me to confirm—I nod my head.

"Layla, Tony was found dead."

She gasps. "What?"

"Around the time you say he left your house and didn't come back. He drown in the Buffalo Bayou."

"Oh my god. I can't believe it." She sounds genuinely surprised.

"We will need to know your exact whereabouts and anyone who you were with," I say.

"Of course. Whatever you need. Tony's dead? I can't believe it. If I had known he was in trouble, I would have reported him missing. I thought he just found another woman to live with."

"He was last at a bar called The Wilde Hare. Have you ever heard of it?" Liam asks.

She searches for any recollection and shakes her head.

"That seems to be the last place Tony was before he died."

"I have never heard of it. And I don't think he ever mentioned going there to me before."

I shove a piece of paper in front of her. Liam and I have fallen into a natural good cop, bad cop scenario.

"Layla," I say, pointing to the paper. "These are text messages from a texting application that had told Tony to meet them at that bar that night."

She glances at the paper and back up at me.

"Is that the texting application you used when y'all first started dating?" I ask.

She shakes her head while looking at the print out showing the phone number. "I'm not sure. I mean..." She trips over her words. "I mean, yes, I used a text app. For safety." She pleads with her eyes. "I don't remember the number, though."

"Layla, take a breath." She does as Liam instructed. "Can you unlock your phone and look?"

Layla does as she is told, but then says, "I don't have the app anymore. I deleted it once we started using regular texts."

Of course.

"Could anyone else have access to that number or application?"

She shrugs and I believe she truly doesn't know the answer. She puts her face in her hands, but doesn't start crying.

"I didn't know anything bad happened to him. I just can't believe this." She lets out a breath. "After he left, I found his criminal record and many women online who said he abused them too." She stares off, lost in her own thoughts.

"Liam will finish getting your statement. If you will excuse me." I'm not sure if she is trying to point us in different directions; I stand before either could say anything else.

Madison

"You okay, man?" The guy sitting on the left side of Chris asks when Chris attempted to go off on him for sitting in the empty seat. He was trying to explain his date, Brianna, was going to join him—however, he was slurring his words already. The guy backs off, I give him a weak smile, as I stand.

"Let's go, Chris," I say as I take him by the arm.

He's too surprised I know his name to protest. Chris wouldn't even look my way the whole time we were sitting at the bar drinking. I tried making small talk, like I have with the others, but he wouldn't even say hello. He let me lead him down the stairs to the bayou with little fight. Maybe it was the extra dose of Rohyphnol I gave him, but this was easier than I expected. The comments on the Facebook group made me think he'd put up a big fight.

This one is one of the evil ones.

He's a MMA fighter in his free time. Takes steroids recre-

ationally. Roid rage is real.

Message me please.

Told me his name was Jason. Ghosted me when I confronted him with his real name based on his phone number, but only after he berated me for calling him out.

Message me, please stay away from him at least.

I heard he got a girl pregnant and beat the baby to death inside her.

When we hung out he'd regularly threaten me saying he was joking. He wasn't joking. I finally was able to find his criminal history and lord let me tell you it was extensive.

I found the same extensive history. Multiple DUIs, assault of a police officer, domestic violence, and possession of a controlled substance; multiple instances of each. Again, I just don't understand how our justice system allows men like this to walk free.

I messaged the multiple women who asked me to—they all had similar stories. Chris met them and quickly love-bombed them into thinking they were the only one. All moved him in quickly, while he was seeing them all at one time. They all experienced him berating them and laying his hands on them. Two of the three women I contacted said he claimed he was infertile but they got pregnant. He insisted the babies weren't his and that they must be the ones cheating, so he beat them until they miscarried. Only one reported the abuse. All the women were scared and embarrassed.

I cannot believe the dating app suggested this man to meet my latest client, Brianna.

"Ultimately, I'm looking for a partnership, mutual connection, where we support each other and grow together. Basically just someone to do life with." Brianna had told me on our video call.

A Texas native, Brianna, is a well-educated project manager making it on her own in Houston. Her long braids and beautiful lashes caught my attention immediately.

"I know they are a lot. Men like to call me high maintenance, but I can afford all this myself and I'm not looking for anyone to fund my lifestyle. Really, I just want someone to share my life with."

Brianna had a genuine warmth to her. I wondered why she was having trouble finding a good partner. I setup her profile right after the call and got inundated with matches and messages.

Message from Chester:

Oh mama! Comesit on my face.

Message from Adam:

Hey beautiful!

Message from Chris:

Hi gorgeous. Let me take you out sometime.

Many more messages just like these came through in response. I messaged as many as I could back to get enough information on them to do research. A lot of them never—Chris, however, kept the conversation going.

Once I had his phone number, I got his full name and address. The photo I uploaded to Facebook produced a lot of comments and then I found his criminal history. I kept the conversation going as Brianna and setup the meeting at the bar on the bayou.

Chris tries to shove me off him when we reach the bottom of the stairs, but he stumbles and loses his balance instead.

"Who are you?" I think is what he is trying to ask, but it comes out as gibberish.

"Chris," I help him up and we start walking down the bayou. "I know who you are and the things you've done. You are an evil, evil man."

He starts to try to speak again, but stumbles again. This time, I don't try to catch him. He almost catches himself, but he can no longer feel his legs, or so it seems. He goes over the edge of the bayou, without any help from me.

Cracking is all I hear until the splash of the water. I'm not sure it was twigs snapping or a bone. I hear nothing, but standing watching the water for a beat too long, silently apologizing to all the women Chris abused.

"HI!" BRIANNA BEAMS.

"Well, hello!" I am surprised at how happy she seems. I was nervous to have this call with her because I haven't found a decent man for her on the dating application. I was getting frustrated but didn't want to set her up with any of the men that matched with her, especially after what happened to Layla with Tony.

"How are you?" She politely asks.

"Who cares? How are you? You are glowing, more than usual."

"Yes, well. Actually, I've been nervous to make this call. I really appreciate all the work you've been doing on the apps for me." She pauses.

I fill the silence. "Yea, of course. I hate it's been taking me so long to find someone decent for even a first date."

I've kept Brianna in the loop about my efforts, sending screenshots of messages as well as what I've found out about the me online—leaving out Chris.

"I know," she sighs. "But I don't need you to keep looking for me."

"Oh?" I don't know if I'm questioning her or surprised or just making a sound for the sake of it.

"Sorry, not because you aren't great. You are amazing." She tries to placate my ego. "I am actually dating someone now."

"Oh?" This time, it's definitely a question.

She smiles. "Yes, so there's this man at work. We have been friends for years, so we know each other really well, even outside of work. He asked me out on an official date a few weeks ago."

I patiently wait for her to tell me more—not filling the silence this time.

"This was actually before I contacted you. But I was keeping my options open. I didn't really know if we could move from friends to more. And we just had the one date. Since then, though, we have gone out a bunch more and officially decided to be exclusive."

"Brianna," I asked in our initial call if she liked to be called anything but Brianna and she told me no—it's always Brianna, and I deeply understand this. "That's so exciting! I am so happy for you!"

"Of course, keep this month's payment, but go ahead and pull my dating profile down."

"I will do that as soon as we hang up. I love this and keep me updated as to how this goes for you!"

"I will!" She promises.

We say goodbye and I am grinning ear to ear, deleting her dating profile. I may not have helped Brianna find love, but I am truly happy for her and hope it all works out exactly how she wants.

Beep. Beep. Beep.

"Hey loves! Your resident ghost dater here. I have missed you all! I am on here today to start helping my forth client! As you women all know, I take to the dating apps for you, I weed through all the candidates, I do throughout research on any man that messages and wants to meet. I only send my clients out with vetted, good quality men. My most recent client has found a great one out in the wild and while I cannot take credit this time, I am still thrilled she is pursuing love. The

next DM after hers will be my next lucky lady! And I will be messaging one of you back today. All my love!" #ghostdater

I don't love the video and look half dead, but I post it anyway. Ellie tells me I need to keep posting and updating people about how ghost dating works, the clients I have helped, and my process. However, I have more comments and messages than I'll ever be able to get through. After my initial video, I gained about 50,000 followers—every video since has gotten me a couple more thousand. Every time I post, I get 50 to 100 new messages. I don't click into each, but I can read the first part of the message through a preview. It's everything from women wanting my help to death threats.

I go down to my last read message, which was Brianna's message. The next one is from a woman with a username of *raedateshouston:*

> Hi! I'm Rae. I'm in my early 30s and struggling to find a good partner out here in HTX. I've only been here for two years. I was previously married to a horrible man who abused me for 10 years. I left him years ago, but it took so long to actually get divorced and actually be rid of him. Way too much information? Oh well, can you help me? I go out, I'm active, live in a great apartment complex in the city, and I've made some great friends, just not a good partner.

Oh Rae, I just hate some men, well people, just mistreat other for their pleasure or because they have unresolved issues they don't want to work on. I message Rae back telling her I will try to help her and the terms to this deal. She messages back immediately agreeing and sets up a video call.

"A body was found in the Buffalo Bayou. l Investigators are on the scene working on identifying the person and what exactly happened. No other information is given as this time."

The video plays on loop—over and over—until the words are ingrained in my soul.

hat, the, hell. Crap! What body was found? What do I do now? Can they link any of the men to me?

I pace my whole apartment, which only takes me about ten steps back and forth. *What am I going to do?* I knew this might be a possibility, but I didn't prepare for it.

Shit! Shit! Shit!

"Honestly, Madison," I start talking to my reflection, standing in front of a small mirror. "There's nothing you can do. It's done. Those men are dead. It happened. And you did it." There's a darkness in my eyes that wasn't there before; I hardly recognize myself.

Detective Oliver

Matthew Parker Day. A 26 year old, white male with short red hair and a steroid problem from Houston, Texas. Matthew was reported missing by his mother—she hadn't heard from him in a few days, which wasn't normal. She made a report with the Montgomery Police Department.

He has six restraining orders against him in Harris County, two in Fort Bend County, and ten in Liberty County. There's reports of abuse, sexual assault, battery, assault with a deadly weapon, and theft. All reports filed by women; no charges or jail time recorded for any of the crimes. I start reading through the reports.

"No one followed up." I say out loud to no one.

"On what?" I nearly pee my pants—Liam a surprise at my door.

"Good God, Liam. Make some noise next time!" I throw a pen at him, he dodges it.

"Sorry, sorry. What are you looking at?" He comes into the office.

"Matthew's record. He has almost two dozen restraining orders against him, countless reports filed. But not a single one of them was followed up on. No other interviews, no photos, no investigation."

"That's so frustrating. I understand why people don't like the police." Liam says.

"And why some take things into their own hands."

"You think a scorned woman killed these men?"

"Well, we know a woman, the same woman, was the last person with each of them. Have we got the footage of Matthew?"

Liam shakes his head. "We haven't been able to connect one woman to all of them. Tony was dating Layla and the other men were talking to different women on the apps."

"We are missing something."

"Of course we are."

We let silence fall between us—*what are we missing here?*

"Oh, Layla told me about this Facebook group?" Liam pulls me out of my thoughts.

"What group?"

"It called something like Are We Doing the Same Guy? I don't know. I have a screen shot of it. Apparently, thousands of women all over the city are on it. They use it to warn each other about terrible men."

"Let me see the screen shot." I open up my personal Facebook account.

"You have a Facebook?" Liam sounds surprised.

"Of course I do. I am of the generation that was one of the first. I remember when you had to have a college email account to sign up." I type in the group name, adding Houston to the end.

"Why would you want to be a part of it though? Wasn't it started to rank women on campuses?"

I shrug. "Everyone was on it. After MySpace, Facebook was the next big social media site."

"Why do you still have it?"

I shrug again. "Does it really matter?"

He laughs. "No, I suppose it doesn't. That's the group."

I have to request to join—questions pop up to answer ensuring that I will not violate the group rules, which include giving away too much information about a man, or telling a man he was posted. I agree to the terms. We could subpoena records from Facebook, but this will be quicker.

I am accepted almost immediately and start scrolling through the posts. Most of them are women post a picture of a man, his initials, asking if anyone has any "tea" on him.

I click on one of the posts. Liam tells me "tea" means gossip or insider information.

Post:

TJ, 32, Beaumont area, any tea

Comments:

Annamarie: This guy has been posted so many times.

Nicole: He looks familiar, DM me.

Charlie: He's married with two children! He works at a nightclub in HTX, security. Always out flirting with any woman who walks in.

Rosa: He looks like a nightmare.

Ivy: I don't know about dating wise but IMO, he sucks as a person. He's just rude & cocky sometimes. Not my cup of tea but he may be yours! Although, his family is AMAZING! Like every human being in his family is truly great!! He just isn't lol.

I close out the post. There's got to be millions of posts just like this one.

"I had no idea something like this existed." Liam says.

"What do you think about it? Like is it valid?" I ask.

"Probably. I have arrested enough terrible men who have committed such heinous crimes against women. If some-one can be saved from just one of them or one instance they might have with them."

I smile at him. Liam is one of the good ones. Then, I smirk, "Wonder if you have been posted?"

He winces. "Kind of."

I laugh. In the search bar, I type in "Liam."

A few posts come up—none of them have Liam's picture attached, nor do any have his correct initials or information. Liam lets out a breath. I laugh again and guess I violated a group rule I initially agreed to uphold.

"Who should we search for first?" I say as I start typing in "Tony" into the search bar.

The first post that pops up has a picture of our first man that went into the bayou, dated around the time it's estimated he went into the water.

"There's 212 comments." I look at Liam, hesitating to open up the comment section.

"I'll get Aida to go through these comments. See if the other men are on here too." Liam says.

I type in each man's name. Each man was posted in this group. Each man has almost 200 comments. I can't imagine they have that many comments in their favor.

"This is a lot of information to shift through." Liam says, almost defeated.

"Yea, have Aida just start going through them. Have IT see if they can track the original poster or posters. I'll have Joe contact Facebook directly for us."

Liam nods and heads out immediately.

I started reading through the comments, even though I thought I'd let Aida handle that, I got curious. So many women accusing these men of terrible things. I am talking about everything from breaking their phones to assaulting their children and everything imaginable in between.

Petal: He's so creepy.

Gerta: This man is on steroids. He thinks he's a big man, but he's a tiny baby.

Julie: Oh, yes. Matthew. He assaulted a child. I called the police and they did nothing. He's a monster, please keep your child away from him. Please just stay away from him.

Amber: I can't believe he allowed to walk the streets. He should be in prison.

Erin: What a joke. Please stay away from this man.

Terra: I worked with him. He's worse than these comments are saying and I only worked with him. I cannot imagine what he's like to date.

Ariel: When on one date with him. He followed me home,

tried forcing himself into my home. Police did nothing. I had to change my phone number and move apartments.

I read a few of these things in the reports filed against Matthew that were never followed up on. I know that as a law enforcer I am supposed to presume innocent until proven guilty, but I believe these women, I believe these reports, I believe Matthew hurt too many women and got away with it.

"Knock knock!" Liam announces himself before entering my office this time. I motion for him to come in and still throw a pen in his direction, just for the sarcasm.

"What's up, Liam?"

"We have a name." He pauses.

"Give me more, Liam."

"A name. One name. Of the single woman who posted each of the Facebook posts."

"One? Really? Already?" He doesn't continue. "Well, what is it?"

"Madison Lily Anderson."

Madison

Rae has a timeless beauty to her, she is also effortless funny—"trauma" she says while laughing at herself. We talked for a bit more about her abusive ex-husband in which she took responsibility for her part in their relationship; she explained she had to move from Chicago to Houston to finally get rid of him and cut her own family off because they were on his side. I believe her when she says she did a lot of work and is ready for a new relationship now, but she's holding back something.

After our video call, she sent me payment for the first month. I created her profile knowing it would get a lot of attention fast. I feel more prepared this time around.

I have followed all news stations and refresh all the pages often. I don't know the process for all that, but so far they haven't released the identity of the body they found. I am sure it's only a matter of time, as these men probably have their fingerprints or DNA in the system, since they were all criminals. I try to not think about the day—I'll have to deal with it then. And until then, I can only keep going on about my business.

As expected, Rae's profile gets so much traction. She has said she hadn't put herself on a dating application, so her ex couldn't find her, but she is ready to stop being afraid of him.

Message from Juan:

> What's up, lil mama?

Message from Cale:

> Good morning, gorgeous.

Message from Matt:

> Hello! I'm not a photographer but I can picture us together.

Message from Gerry:

> I bet your vagina tastes like fowers.

Message from Corey:

> Hello! You are gorgeous!

Message from Kent:

> Can you suck it? Good?

Gross! These men can be so gross! There is about 15 other messages just like these. I start going through each profile, slowly—I take notes on each man and gather enough from their profile to make a judgment about them. I also decide to reply to each one of them to see which one replies and to see if any of these men are as terrible as Tony, Mark, or Chris.

I thought I was only a ghost dater, chasing love for women. But I've become a ghost maker, too, silencing men for women.

I JOLT AWAKE IN a cold sweat, my whole body soaked. *What happened?* It takes a moment to realize I had been asleep. I was only dreaming. Tony, or a figure that vaguely looked like Tony, was chasing me down the bayou. The water rushing, calling my name in a faint whisper.

It was just a dream, Madison. I grab some ice water from the kitchen.

What are you doing? You are a murderer. Like you actually have killed people. Multiple people. How did I even get here? This is who I am now? This is who I am now.

Instead of getting back to bed, I sit down at my computer. I type in the search bar: body found in the bayou Houston

No new articles come up. I guess they haven't identified the body. I don't know if it is Tony, Mark, or Chris. Maybe it is none of them and is someone else entirely.

Next I search each man's name. No missing person reports seem to be filed for any of them. It hits me—most people use Facebook for these things now.

Navigating to a new tab, I type in Facebook. Once it loads, I type in each man's name again, one-by-one. The only thing that pops up is their pages. I click on each opening in a new tab. Slowly, I go through friends lists, looking first for potential family members.

Tony doesn't seem to have any family on his friends list—which doesn't surprise me.

I type in Mark's real name into the search bar. His page is public, but there isn't much posted. I quickly find a few people with his same last name. Most of those profiles are private, however, there is one woman. This must be his sister and she posts excessively. Scrolling, I learn she has three kids, I know their habits, hobbies, and schools. There's little evidence Mark is even related. I find one photo she posted two years ago of them when they were kids. She captioned it "Look at those babies!"

Chris's family was easier to find, as he had them all tagged and linked right on his page. Clicking through each, I find very little about Chris. His mom's page is public and for a brief second my heart drops thinking about a mother losing their child. But I cannot find any evidence on her page of having any children.

It doesn't seem like there is anyone out there missing these men. *Does this confirm I did the right thing?*

"Hey!" I slide into the chair next to Matt.

"Oh, uh. Hey?" He stumbles and spills his drink. This one is clumsy before the drugs, may be easier than expected.

"Woah, big boy."

"Ah. Sorry." He says as the bartender tries to clean up the mess.

"Let me get you another," I offer.

"No, it's fine. Do I know you?" He looks up at me—trying to place where he's seen my face.

"I don't think so." I put my hand out for him to shake. "Stephanie."

He takes my hand, "Matt."

Matt orders himself another drink and goes to the restroom to clean himself up. While he's gone, I slip the Rohyphol in his glass. Easy, peasy. These men should really start watching out for their unattended drinks, like women have to.

I recently saw an advertisement for a drink cover that seals the top of the cup, to prevent drugs being slipped in. It was advertised to both women and men; however, something tells me men don't think about this happening as often as women do.

I push his glass near him when he sits back down. I hold my glass to cheers and he follows suit.

After a long gulp, he says, "I don't know why I even ordered this, clearly I'm being stood up."

"Oh, man. That sucks. I'm sorry."

Silence lingers between us.

"I mean you can still make the best of the night. You look great, might as well take advantage." I finally say, holding up my glass again. He cheers again and takes another long gulp.

"You are very pretty, Stephanie."

Chills shoot down my spine. Matt is giving me the creepiest grin I've ever seen—it's not flattering at all. Now I understand some of the comments from my Facebook post asking for information about Matt.

He's so creepy. Will hit on anything that walks.

I think my sister dated him years ago, he was weird and creepy. Forced her into a BDSM type relationship.

**Trigger warning* This man is a ped, he has slept with 13 year olds, 15, and 17 year olds. He even admitted to me he's slept with his own family members. Be careful if you run into him.*

"Oh, thanks," I try my best to make myself blush and fake being flattered by his compliment.

"You came here alone?"

"Yea. I love this little place. Tell me about this," I gingerly touch the tattoo on his bicep; he immediately flexes.

"Oh, it was literally a drunken thing I did months ago. Went in blitzed, picked it out from the wall. Bastards didn't want to tattoo me, but I forced them to."

"Do you often force people into doing what you want?"

"You want to find out?"

"Oh, Matt. What do you want to force me do?" I try to sound flirty, but I just want to vomit.

"Well," he gives me look, "for starters..." Thankfully, he's interrupted.

"Y'all want anything else?" A bartender with short, dark hair and striking green eyes, asks.

I shake my head, knowing I've already paid cash for the drink I didn't drink. Matt orders one more and closes his tab. He should be feeling not only the drugs, but the alcohol soon. The bartender puts the drink between us, as I hand it to Matt, I slip more drugs in the glass.

Matt is not a little guy in terms of height and he definitely goes extra hard in the gym. I wouldn't be surprised if he was also on steroids like Chris.

"What do you say, after this," he picks up his glass, "We get out of here." It should be a question, but Matt says it as a statement. He's also started slurring his words.

"Yes, big guy. Let's get out of here." I wink. "So hurry up."

This gets him going, but he struggles to pick up his glass—it feels like it's hundred pounds. Using both hands, confused, he finally picks it up and downs the drink.

"Don..." I assume he's trying to say he is done while struggling to get up from his chair.

"I got you, Matt." I help him up, stabilizing him under his right arm. His legs wobble. I lead him to the door—people are watching a sick, now small woman, practically carry this man.

"Where, we," Matt tries to speak again, but still can't get words out.

"Shhhh." I put my finger on his lips, as we stumble down the ramp to the Brays Bayou.

After the news story of the body found in the Buffalo Bayou, I needed to change my scenery. I scouted this bar out a few days ago—I didn't actually go inside, but walked to the bayou from the parking lot. I also noted the bayou was swollen, water pressing against it's edges, almost over-spilling.

His legs give way and I can't keep holding him up any-more—my muscles burn and pulse under his weight. I let him fall to the ground and he grunts as he slams against the cement.

"Shhh."

He tries speaking again or maybe is just trying to make sounds as he's trying to get back up on his feet. His body fails him as he slips back to the ground.

"Shut up! Geez." I'm getting annoyed as he is making more sounds. We are alone, I look up and down the bayou to double-check. It's dark down here and anyone could sneak up on us. He grunts again, louder.

"Just get out of here." I bend down and push Matt. He grabs my arm—*how does his still have this much strength?*

"Let's go!" I say through clenched teeth. One by one, I pull each one of his fingers off my arm—he doesn't try to grab me again.

One more shove and he's over the edge. He tries scream-ing, louder this time. I hear him scraping the concrete wall that lines the bayou, then flailing as he struggles. He gargles water, trying to survive. While full, this bayou's water isn't rushing like the other one had been. I stand there in the darkness until silence folds around me save for the cicadas' low, electric hymn.

"Hey girl!" Ellie is cheerful this evening.

I, on the other hand, am exhausted. I met Matt three days ago and I haven't slept since. I hear the sound of water going into his throat every time I close my eyes.

"Hi."

"You look tired," Ellie says.

"I haven't slept much the last few days."

"Madison, you need to take care of yourself!"

Air hisses between my teeth. *I'm dying anyway—well, we all are, aren't we?*

"Are you taking your medication?" she finally asks.

"Yes," I lie and bite the inside of my upper lip. I hate lying to her and I know she means well, I just wish she would leave it alone.

"Good. I'm worried with everything coming back, I'm going to lose you soon. Your medication should be helping. You've lost a lot of weight though." She says the last part as a judgment, not just an observation.

"I know, Ellie, I'm fine. It will all be fine."

"How's the ghost dating business?"

"It's kind of exhausting. And Ellie, these men out here are so horrible! Worse than Tony. If you can imagine."

"Really?! I didn't think they could get any worse than him!"

"Me either! But they are. I mean I came across a man who beat his pregnant girlfriend." I pause. "She lost the baby. And another man who admitted to raping children and family members."

Ellie gasps.

"I'm sorry, Ellie. I shouldn't have said that."

"It's okay. I just can't believe evil like that exists out there."

Well, that particular evil does not exist in the world, any more.

"I know! And just out there walking free able to hurt other people."

We let the injustice cling to the air, turning silence into near suffocation. If she only knew—*would Ellie be proud of me for getting rid of the vile? Or would she be appalled I am a murderer?*

"How is this pregnancy for you?" I ask.

Ellie lights up again—like I hoped it would.

"This second trimester has been so great, thankfully after such an awful first one."

"So glad!"

"Yea, I've been able to get her room ready and still run around with Jess."

"What do you still need for her?"

"Nothing. Poor girl is just getting Jess's old things. Ouch!" Ellie grabs her stomach. "She just kicked me hard."

"Oh geez, Ellie."

"No, it's so awesome to feel them inside you, moving all around. I can't wait for you to experience this one day."

"No thank you." I shake my head. Ellie knows I never would have been able to have kids anyway. "You know they should have taken my ovaries a long time ago. I might not be sick now if they had?"

Ellie knows that I'm right; having a rare ovarian cancer at a young age only increases the risk of it coming back or a new version forming inside me. They didn't want to because "what if you want kids one day?" the doctor had asked. My dad pushed for me to keep my reproductive organs that were slowly killing me. He was my guardian, so I guess that meant he got control of *my* body.

"Does Kevin want kids?" I wish she would leave Kevin out of this.

"No, he doesn't."

Ellie wrinkles her nose and furrows her brows. "Really?" She can't imagine how anyone wouldn't want to have kids. Ellie always wanted to be a mother and she's great at it, as I knew she would be.

"Yea, something we agree on for sure."

"Well, I wish y'all would agree on coming up to see us, so we can finally meet him."

"We will be up when the baby is born. I promise."

"You really promise?"

"Pinkie promise."

We hold up our pinkies to the camera. Something we have done since we met—pinkie promises are not meant to be broken, ever. I hope I can keep part of this one.

Detective Oliver

Madison Lily Anderson. A quick search tells us she is a 34 year old woman, who moved to Houston in 2012, but grew up in Blanding, Utah. After high school graduation, she attended University of Kentucky. She has no criminal record and according to her most recent driver's license, she is 5'5", 161 pounds, blonde, with blue eyes.

While most of her social media accounts leave a lot to the imagination, they are all public. The photos of Madison on Facebook, fit the grainy videos we have of the woman leading the men outside of The Wilde Hare.

"Boss," Liam calls to me across the conference room.

Aida, Liam, and I have over taken the room now that we might have an actual lead in these cases.

"Don't. I am not your boss." I retort.

"Yea, it sounded weird coming out my mouth."

Aida giggles. Aida doesn't say much, she mostly has her face glued to her computer, but she sure is giggly.

"I was just going trough Madison's TikTok account. She has these videos explaining she is offering a ghost dating service for women."

"Ghost dating? What does that mean?"

"Apparently, she gets on the dating app for women, she does all the swiping and initial conversations. Then, when she thinks she found a good match, she gives the woman the information and lets her meet the man."

"Hm. Interesting."

"I'm going through these comments to see if I can find any of the women our men were talking to or supposed to meet the night they died."

On a white board, we have each man's name, picture, and basic information. Under each, is the name of the woman he was meeting the night he was led to his death in the bayou.

Tony - Layla

Tomas - Clare

Chris - Brianna

Matthew - Rae

"Y'all?" Aida says. We look at her to continue. "We just got the bar's footage of Matthew."

She projects the video on the screen in the room. We watch each clip that was send to Aida—Jamal, the bar manager, sent over the full footage from the day; IT sifted through it for us. The first video shows Matthew entering the bar. This footage is in color, although it is nighttime, so it's still hard to see all the details.

The second video, a white woman enters the bar, who looks similar to our Madison—she appears to have lost a significant amount of weight though. No one says anything as we watch the next video—this one is inside the bar. This one is less helpful. It shows the back right of two people sitting at the bar. The people appear to be Madison and Matthew, however, it is difficult to say for certain.

This video continues, it appears as if they were talking and having a good time together. Each one gets up, the man stumbles, the woman helps him. The video cuts out. Finally, a video shows the couples back as they exit the bar to the parking lot. They pause, talking for a minute, she readjusts holding him up, and then they walk off, towards the bayou.

"Bingo." I say triumphant.

"You think it's really her?" Liam asks.

"I do." I say while nodding my head.

"You want to pay her a visit?" Liam asks.

"What else do we know about her? Family here?"

Aida shakes her head. "All her family is in Utah. I'm not finding many relatives though, her dad is there."

"I want a little more before we make any moves on her." I tell them; they nod and get back to work.

We sit in silence, working, trying to find out as much about Madison as we can.

"How about this?" Liam finally says. "I.T. just emailed."

We all click over to our emails. The secure text message application finally released records. All the numbers that were texting these men, were Madison. Each one setup with her email and information.

"It's got to be her." Liam says.

"I agree, let's go pay her a visit." We all three abandon our computers and work.

"Madison, police." Liam knocks on her door. No one answers. He knocks again and again.

"I'll go see if the property manager is still here." Aida says.

I try peering through a window—there's nothing to see. A few minutes later, a small, angry woman carrying a key follows Aida from the leasing office.

"This is Marie. She says Madison turned in her notice to vacate a few days ago. She's not sure if she is still here anymore." Aida says. I try introducing Liam and I, but Marie waves us off.

She opens the door to the apartment. Liam draws his gun, again announcing that the police are here. He walks through, ensuring the place is clear. The place is entirely clear. It doesn't appear as if anyone has lived here in a while. It's spotless; the crisp, chemical bite of bleach hitting me the moment I step in.

"When did she turn in her notice to vacate?" I ask Marie.

"Two days ago." She grabs the keys sitting on the counter. "Couldn't even turn in her keys herself, I see." She rolls her eyes.

"I really wish you hadn't picked those up." Liam says. "We will need you finger prints, now."

"Ughhh," she drags out the sound like we have ruined her entire existence.

"Did you have a professional cleaner come in here?" I ask.

"No, we do that when someone has officially moved out. We didn't know she left already, just that she was going to at the end of her lease."

"When is the end of her lease?"

"She's got two more months."

"Did she give a forwarding address?"

"Nope. We still needed to do a walk through with her, but we hadn't because she was supposed to stay for a few more months."

We do another sweep of the apartment. It looks like she either had someone else clean the place, or she bleached the whole place herself before leaving.

Liam and Aida finish the conversation with Marie about Madison and what she knew about her—from what I overhear, not much. She was a model tenant; always paid rent on time, kept to herself, caused no issues.

They knock on a few of Madison's neighbors doors. Only one person answers and they had no idea anyone even lived in apartment 113.

I stand looking out at the parking lot.

Where are you Madison?

Madison works as an accountant at a technology company with an office space located downtown Houston. The drive from her apartment to downtown takes almost an hour, and it's not even rush hour—I bet the drive in the morning and evenings were brutal. I don't understand how people do it every day.

"Hi, I'm Rowan. I believe I spoke to you." A tall woman stands before us; she turns toward Liam. Liam nods and takes her hand in his.

"Yes, it was me. Thank you for meeting us. This is Detective Oliver." Liam introduces me to the woman; we shake hands and she leads us to a conference room.

This room is floor to ceiling windows, there is no privacy here—I can see everyone's eyes on us, whispering about who we are and why we are here. Rowan motions for us to sit, as she takes a seat opposite the table. Her skin is a rich, deep brown that glows under the light.

"Detectives, what can I help you with?" Rowan starts the conversation. "You were pretty vague on the phone."

"Ma'am, you were Madison Anderson's immediate supervisor?" Liam asks.

She nods her head. "Is everything okay with Madison? I've been pretty worried about her."

"What makes you worried about her?" I ask.

"She quit very abruptly a few days ago. No notice, didn't want to have a conversation with me about it. Just said she was done here. Turned in her computer and left." Rowan shakes her head. I raise my eyebrow at Liam.

"How long did she work here?"

"I think it was just at two years."

"What kind of employee was she?"

"The easy kind. I never had any issues with her, she kept to herself mostly, but came in and did good work."

"So her quitting seemed…" Liam starts asking, but trails off to let Rowan fill in the blank.

"Definitely out of the blue. She seemed happy here. I asked where she was going, which company stole her from me. I offered her more money, but she said that wasn't the issue. I seriously don't know." She shrugs, defeated by the situation.

"Did you know her beyond your working relationship?"

She shakes her head. "No, I didn't. Madison was really private. She never came out to company events, no happy hours, nothing. However, she did talk to her pod mate, Lauri."

"Pod mate?" I interrupt.

"Oh yes, we call the groups of desks pods. So the people sitting around you are pod mates." She laughs. "I think Robbie also forced himself on her too."

"I'm sorry? A man named Robbie forced himself on her?" I raise my eyebrow so high, it might jump off my forehead.

"Oh sorry, not like that." She waves her hands in front of her as if she can wipe away the words. "He forced a friendship with her. He is overly friendly with everyone."

"Do you think he would have harmed her in any way?" I have to ask.

"Oh, no! Robbie is harmless! No one here would harm anyone in any way."

"Do you know where we could find Madison?"

"No. I mean she isn't here, obviously. So at home?" She shrugs.

"Thanks." I say curtly.

"Can we talk to Lauri and Robbie and anyone else Madison might have worked closely with?" Liam asks.

"Of course, I'll go get Lauri first." She leaves us.

Liam sighs. "So she left her apartment, she quit her job. What is she doing? You think she ran? Does she know we are onto her?"

A knock on the glass door vibrates the wall of glass. Liam waves the small woman inside.

"I'm Lauri. Rowan said you wanted to talk to me?" She has a presence that is commanding.

Liam and I both stand; I introduce us, we shake hands, and sit.

"Lauri, we understand you were close to Madison Anderson?"

"I wouldn't say close." She answers.

"What would you say?"

"We worked together and were friendly while here. But I don't even think I have her personal number."

"I see. Y'all didn't go anywhere together outside of work?"

"We. Madison, Robbie, and I would go to lunch sometimes. Is everything okay with Madison?"

"We are trying to locate her."

"Is she in trouble?"

"We just need to ask her some questions."

"I wish I could help. But like I said, I don't even have her number. She quit a few days ago." She snaps her fingers. "Gone, just like that. She didn't even tell me she was quitting before, she told Rowan it was her last day, and was just gone after lunch one day."

"Thank you, Lauri. If you hear anything from Madison, will you let us know?"

She agrees and leaves the conference room. I watch as she takes a seat at a desk only ten feet from the room. A tall, lanky man is standing at her desk with eyes wide. They exchange words and then he heads straight into the room, no knock first.

"Hi! I'm Robbie." He sits before we could get up.

Liam introduces us, no handshake.

"I was Madison's best friend." He laughs. "I wasn't but I wanted to be."

"Can you tell us the nature of your relationship?"

Robbie's face scrunches, annoyed with our formality.

"We worked together. I tried my best being her friend. I was helping her plan her wedding."

"Wedding? She is engaged?"

"Oh yes. To the wonderful Kevin." Robbie talks more with his hands than his words.

"Have you met Kevin?"

"No, no. Madison keeps everything close to the chest. I only heard about him from her."

"Oh. When was the last time you saw her?"

"I guess the day she quit."

"Did you know she was planning on quitting?"

He shakes his head and gives the same story Lauri did. We explain we are looking to speak to her and if he hears from her to let us know. He seemed more eager to help than anyone else we have talked to so far. No one at the company could give us any more information on Madison.

Who are you, Madison?

"What the hell is this about?" Madison's father, Francious Anderson, yells in the phone after it's first ring. Thankfully, we have him on speaker phone in the conference room and he is not yelling in my ear.

"I am Detective Oliver with the Houston Police Department. I was hoping to talk to you about your daughter, Madison." I say calmly, trying not to match his tone.

"Is she in trouble?" He asks, lowering his tone this time.

"We are trying to figure that out, sir. When is the last time you talked to her?" I ask.

"I don't even know. I keep calling her but she doesn't answer my phone calls. I haven't seen her since she moved to that god forsaken town."

"She hasn't been to Utah recently?"

"Nope. She refuses. Won't even come back when I told her, her uncle needed her."

"Her uncle, that's your brother?"

"Yea. He always saw her as her as his own daughter. Especially after what happened to his own son. But she doesn't care. Not about him. Not about me."

"I'm sorry. What happened to his son?"

"Oh he died. Years ago. You would think after her mother died she would care more about family." There's bitterness in his voice, but there's something more too.

"Again, I'm sorry. We couldn't find much information abut Madison's mother."

"She killed herself. When Madison was a baby."

"I'm so sorry for your loss. Both of them."

"She was a bitch. Blamed me."

"Who?"

"Her mother. Well, Madison is a bitch too. Blames me for everything wrong in her life. Her mother killing herself. Her struggles. Every damn thing."

"Can I ask how your nephew died?"

"He killed himself too. In my own damn house."

"Do you know anyone who might help us locate her? We weren't able to find her at her apartment or work."

"Well she for damn sure isn't here!" He is yelling again.

"I understand sir, but is there anyone who might help us locate her?"

"Maybe that one bitch. Oh what was her name? The only person she really talks to or about. Um…" He stutters. "Emmie, no. Ellie. That's it. She doesn't tell me much but I remember her yelling at me that this Ellie is her only real family."

"Thank you so much, sir. You have been helpful. If Madison does turn up or reaches out, can you call us?" I lie, he hasn't been much help—he doesn't even have Ellie's information, and I don't think he will call us back if he does hear from her.

"I guess." He sighs and hangs up.

Madison

Beep. Beep. Beep.

"*Hi y'all! I…uh…uh. Ugh!*" Delete.

Beep. Beep. Beep.

"*Hi y'all! As always I wanted to jump on to give an update. Things are going. It's so hard out here! Kudos to those pushing through, dating, using the apps all yourself. Like y'all are some champs. I am currently working with my forth client. She has went on a few dates and has a potential match that I'm excited for. Hopefully, that means I can start working on helping another woman get off these apps! I wish I could help more than one woman at a lime and maybe one day I can.*" I take a deep breath. "*It would just be too much right now. Keep looking for love beautiful people.*" #ghostdater

I blow a kiss to the camera before collapsing in complete exhaustion.

Comments:

Milo Mango: She looks ill.

Shadow Runner Joe: Have you slept?
CupcakeJessie: Keep up the good work girl.
Theo: Seriously fat bitch. Just shut up.
ElleNova: Love you girl! You are doing amazing!
KimPossible: Just stop now!
Maxie Steele: What is this bullshit.
Kitty Kat: Oh my gosh, it's so rough out there.
TiffTreats_999: You are doing amazing.
Aria Whispers 213: Love this! This is genius.
Seven Blazer: Stop catfishing people.
Clare: So glad I found you!

I normally don't read comments, I'm not even sure why I am now. I close the application—this is getting to be a lot.

How can I continue on like this? Should I just quit now?

I sit on my bed, heart racing, sweat dripping down my back. Scrubbing an apartment from top to bottom is more challenging than pushing a man in the bayou.

I spoke with the building manager yesterday, told her I would not be renewing my lease once it is up in two months. She wanted me to give her a forwarding address, not just for my mail but in case they need to bill me for repairs they need to do once I leave—I couldn't give her one, I don't know where my car will end up taking me until my unavoidable death, which will come soon. I'm getting weaker and sicker. I stopped going to doctor appointments, there's no reason to go anymore.

I started packing up the contents of my life in Houston. There's a suitcase full of enough clothes for the next few months. There's a few trash bags headed to the dumpsters. There's a few boxes set for donations going to the local women's shelter. There's nothing to keep.

A journal sticks out of one of the trash bags—the blue, floral design reminds me it's full of poems, stories, quotes from high school. I pull it out, flipping to a random page:

But now I'm ripping off your mask, revealing the real you. I watch it melt off, like the covers of burning books.

My heart leaps as the phone rings.

"Hi, Madison!" Rae's face lights up the screen.

"Hi, Rae. How are you?"

"I'm great. How are you?"

"I'm good." I exhale, long and heavy. I hope she doesn't pat attention to my exasperation and continues the conversation. She texted me two days ago wanting to talk; I have no idea what about.

"Are you sure?" She asks.

I chuckle. "Yes, just stressed at work." I don't know if she believes me.

"I'm sorry. I hope it gets better."

"Thanks, what's up with you?"

She takes a deep breath. "I think you can go ahead and take my dating profile down."

"Oh yea?" I'm genuinely surprised I'm losing another client so soon.

"Not that I'm committing to any one person right now. I just don't want my profile out there or any more dates for the apps."

I want her to tell me more, but I don't know what to ask. My brain is flooded with every thought imaginable, but it's also empty.

She continues on her own. "I'm still dating a few of the men you sent over."

"Can I ask who?"

"Yea, Corey and Nick. But I've also been exploring myself. Solo dates, finding new hobbies, taking new fitness classes. Those kinds of things."

"That's great!"

"Yea, I feel more like myself, finally. Of course I can date and do all those things and continue being myself. I just don't feel like I need the dating apps to find someone, or to meet new people right now."

"Of course, that makes sense. I am so happy you are discovering yourself more. I hope you continue to do so. And the person for you will come along when you need them."

"Yea," she smiles.

"Keep me updated, Rae. With the men and you."

"I will. I hate I won't be officially working with you anymore. But I'm glad you get to move onto help someone else."

"Oh for sure!"

We say our goodbyes. I truly am happy for her. You really need to find yourself, love yourself before you can bring someone else into your life. Probably why I've never let anyone into my life.

I click open Facebook; blood drains from my face—*oh shit.*

Detective Oliver

Ellie Marie Paster was Madison's college roommate. Thankfully, her information was easy to find. She still lives in Kentucky—somehow I was able to convince Joe to allow me and Liam to fly up to meet Ellie in person and see if that's where Madison ran off to. James wasn't too happy for this impromptu trip, which meant we had to miss a doctor's appointment.

"I just want to make sure everything is okay for her in there." He pleaded as I packed a small bag to carry on the plane with me.

"I know. Me too. But we have got to catch this woman. James, you know it's important."

He sighed. "I know. I'm just worried about the two of you." He deflated on the bed.

I sat next to him, hugging him from the side, laying my head on his chest. "We'll be okay. I promise."

He put his hand on my belly. "She kicked!" He jumped up with joy—she did not kick. "I felt her kick!" He danced around the room.

I haven't felt her kick yet, but I hear it's hard to feel it early on and especially since this is my first pregnancy. Well, my first that made it this far. I don't have the heart to tell James she didn't kick, so I let him have the moment.

"How do you feel about flying?" Liam asks as we find our seats.

"I don't mind it. I mean take off and landing are always a bit rough, but," I end my sentence with a shrug.

"Would it surprise you to know I hate it?"

I laugh. It absolutely does *not* surprise me that Liam hates flying.

"Just breathe. And here, chew on this." I hand him a piece of gum.

The plane ride from Houston to Kentucky takes about three hours. In that time I have reviewed some questions we prepared in case Madison isn't with her friend. Liam is hopeful, I am less optimistic. That, too, tends to be our dynamic.

Liam grips the seat in front of him as we make our landing. He braces for impact that doesn't come.

"You survived." I tease. He doesn't find it funny.

We grab our things and deplane. An officer is waiting on us. Normally, we would just send a local police officer to check on a suspect or their friends or family in another state, but considering this is an active serial killer case—they allowed us to come question Ellie in person. And to see if this is where our number one suspect ran off to.

"Detectives. I'm Officers Flores, just call me Ana." We shake hands, introducing ourselves as well. Ana has coarse, long black hair twisted into a low bun and there's a quiet authority in the way she holds herself.

"My captain caught me up on the details of your case. Well, the details you shared with her. I'll say it's not a lot." Ana says as we climb into her squad car.

"Yea. I think you understand we have to keep this one close. We seem to have an active serial killer on the run." I say.

"And you think she is here?"

Liam and I exchange a look.

"We will find out. All we know is her closest friend is out here. So even if she isn't here, we hope to find out more about our suspect."

"I understand. I've got her address, ready?"

We nod and are on our way. Almost an hour in the car and we finally arrive at Ellie's house. We park in front of a row of similar town homes.

"Ana? Can you knock on some neighbors doors and see if they have seen Madison? You should have a current image of her." She nods and walks to the next house over.

Liam and I knock on Ellie's front door. Immediately, a white man in his mid-thirties answers the door while a screaming toddler runs away into another room, slamming the door. *Oh man, they start slamming doors that early?!*

"Oh." The man says—we clearly caught him off guard.

"Hi. I'm Detective Oliver and this is Detective Callahan. May we come in? We have some questions for you Mr. Porter and your wife."

"Oh. Um." He stutters, but doesn't move.

"Mr. Porter, is Madison Anderson here?" I ask.

"Madison? No why would she be here?"

"We are looking for her and understand Mrs. Porter is her friend."

"Yea. Uh. Come in." He finally moves so we can enter. Both Liam and I start scoping out the place. Immediately inside the door is a small foyer, we see four closed doors. Nick opens one of the doors and we instinctively follow.

"Oh, give me a second to make sure my daughter is in bed for her nap." Liam was closest to the bedroom door, he peers inside; looking back at me he shakes his head.

"Mind if I look around down here?" Liam asks.

"Go ahead. Now Miss Jess!" His tone changes with his audience.

Liam opens the next door, it's another bedroom. There's a crib and some paint samples. I put my hand on my belly. Soon a room in my house will look like this one.

Liam checks the closet, there's only some baby clothes hanging in the lonely dark, space. I open the next door, it's a small bathroom and nothing more.

"Alright, let's head up." Nick says, closing the little girl's door behind him.

"Mind if I check this last door first?" Liam asks.

"It's just a very messy garage, but go ahead."

"Mr. Porter, we can head up." I follow him upstairs.

"Call me Nick. Hey, El!" He says when we are halfway up the stairs.

The top of the stairs open up to a kitchen, dining room, and living room. This house has a modern, open floor plan. To the left is an open door. I can barely see anything but it looks like it's the primary suite.

"Oh." Ellie is startled by the presence of an officer in her house.

"Hi, Mrs. Porter. I'm Detective Oliver." I put my hand out for her to shake—she does, looking wearily at her husband.

"Can I look in this room?" Nick motions to allow me to.

"I don't know, babe. They mentioned Madison?" I hear Nick say to Ellie.

"What about her?" She asks.

I move into the room, checking the closet and bathroom. There is no sign of Madison or anyone else, besides the family, in the house. By the time I am back in the living room, Liam has made it up the stairs—he gives me a head shake. So, he didn't find anything either. Ellie is completely shook up.

"We apologize for just coming here unannounced. Can we sit and talk?" I ask.

"Of course. Nick said you asked about Madison?" Ellie asks as she takes a seat at the dining room table.

"Yes, we understand you are friends with Madison Anderson."

"I am. We are best friends." She shifts uncomfortably. "Oh god. Has something happened? She can't be dead yet.

She has a few more months." Tears streak her face and Nick reaches for his wife's hand.

"I'm sorry, what?" It's Liam that can ask before I can.

"Please tell me she is still alive," Ellie pleads.

"Why would you think she is dead?" I ask.

"Because she's sick. She doesn't have much time left."

"We think she is still alive, ma'am. And we are trying to locate her. Would she be in a hospital? In hospice care?" Liam asks.

"No, Madison didn't want all that. Wants to just let death take her when it does, where it does." She wipes her tears. "You really think she is still alive,"

"We hope so."

"Can you try to call her and see if she will tell you where she is? Don't tell her Houston police are looking for her," I ask.

She nods and gets her phone from the kitchen counter. The phone doesn't even ring once. It goes straight to voicemail. It might be dead or turned off. She hasn't canceled her cell service, yet, we know that much.

"Thank you for trying." Liam says.

Ellie's worry washes over her face, again.

"Can you tell us about Madison and your friendship?"

She nods. Ellie starts with how her and Madison met freshman year and became fast friends; how she stayed in Kentucky but Madison ventured out on her own, making her way to Houston.

Ellie tells us about Madison's strained relationship with her father, with her family—which is as we already knew just her dad and uncle. She mentions she had a cousin that passed after freshman year.

"Madison changed after that." Ellie took a breath, finally.

"What do you mean?" I ask.

She shrugs. "She seemed...lighter, happier? Maybe?"

What an interesting thing to say. Why would someone seem happier after the death of a family member—especially the second in her very small family.

We finally made it back to the topic of Madison's illness—we are careful not to ask too many questions, but know we can pull her medical records when we get back home.

"She got sick as a teenager. A rare ovarian cancer. Her dad didn't do the best job taking care of her after her mom died, but he surprisingly took care of that. It went away but came back in a different form more recently. She refused care this time. Just wants to succumb to death." She sounds sad, disappointed, and a little bit angry.

"I'm sorry you are having to watch your friend go through something so horrible. It's challenging." I say with as much empathy as I can.

"You're pregnant? How far along?" She rubs her belly and I realize I had my hand on my stomach as soon as she started talking about Madison's illness. I don't want to imagine watching my daughter go through ovarian cancer, or any cancer for that matter.

"Sorry," she says. "I shouldn't have assumed. I hated when people would assume I was pregnant, even when I was or am." Ellie has a visible pregnant belly, but like she said, no one wanted to assume.

I wave her off. "Yes, I'm having a girl. My first baby."

She smiles. "This is our second girl. You are going to be a great mom. I can tell." I tear up—I refuse to cry about anything, but especially at work.

Liam sees my struggle and chimes in, "Ellie, thank you so much for speaking with us today. We really appreciate it."

"You never said why you are looking for Madison." Ellie says.

"We can't really discuss details. But she is a person of interest in a few cases are working on." Liam says.

"Like she witnessed something?"

"We can't really say much more. We would really appreciate it, though, if you hear from her if you would reach out to us." Liam hands her a card with his information on it.

"Um. Yea, I guess."

I don't believe her. Ellie seems like a loyal friend over anything else. I think she'll warn Madison we are on to her—we have to find her first.

"Please excuse me." Liam holds up his ringing phone, stands, and moves to the hallway.

Ellie continues to talk to me about being a girl-mom and gushing about the joys and the struggles of motherhood. I tried to pay attention but I am also trying to overhear Liam's phone call too.

Liam hangs up and walks back over to us. "I'm sorry, but Oliver, we need to go."

Once we are out the door and back at Ana's car, I look at Liam to tell me what happened and why we are leaving so abruptly. He doesn't read my body language.

"What's going on, Liam?" I finally ask.

"A man was attacked last night. At the Brays Bayou. He survived, in the hospital now. There's a witness." Liam finally says, giving little detail.

"Did the victim give a statement? What did the witness see? Was it Madison?" I ask in quick succession.

"Possibly. Aida said the witness's statement matches Madison's description. The victim is still unconscious. I asked Aida to call Twist and Tonic to see if the victim was there before he was attached at the bayou."

"Hey, none of the neighbors have seen Madison here," Ana joins us at the car.

I shake my head. "Yea, she definitely isn't here. We got to go!" She didn't ask questions, just drove us back to the airport.

Madison

Top headline of all the local news stations I follow: *Houston Man Missing.*

Oh shit. Oh shit. Oh shit.

I stare at the headline for 20 minutes without opening any article. Months ago I started following all of the local stations, waiting for this very moment. I thought I'd be more prepared for it.

It might not even be one of the men, Madison. You have to open an article to find out. There's millions of people in this city and many go missing everyday, you have to find out if it's one of the men or not.

Matthew Parker Day, 26 has been reported missing by his family. He was last seen March 21st at work. He also has not been heard from since. If you have any information or see Mr. Day, please alert authorities.

My vision blurs, I wobble on my feet.

How did I get on the bathroom floor? I wipe the drool from the side of my mouth. *Did I actually end up passing out?* But how did I end up in the bathroom—I am pretty sure I was in my bedroom.

Missing Houston Man—headlines storm my thoughts. That's right.

What the fuck am I going to do?

Just breathe, Madison. All you can do is breathe.

No one saw you guys together. I mean, no a whole bar full of people saw you together, but they won't remember, *right?* Matt looks like a very generic white man—even if they remember a drunk man stumbling out of the bar, they won't recognize Matt. He looked like every other guy there.

They won't recognize me either, right? I look at myself in the mirror. *God, you look terrible; those circles under your eyes are so dark and your face is so sunken.* I run my fingers through my hair and more strands than normal come out between my fingers.

Yup, just a generic, white woman, who looks a little tired, sick maybe, but definitely just a generic white woman.

I used cash at the bar, so they can't track me or my name that way, and I always give a fake name. No way. No way they can trace me to Matt or Matt to me.

It will be okay. It will all be okay. Just breathe.

"Layla!" I force a smile from the unexpected call.

"Hey, Madison." Her smile is forced too.

"What's up?" I ask, hesitantly.

"Tony is dead," she says flatly.

"What?" I try to sound as shocked as I can, she seems to buy it—maybe I should have been an actress, I almost laugh out loud at the thought.

"I just left the police station."

Shit, I guess it was his body they found.

"Did you hear from him after he left that day?" I ask her.

"No, you said to block him, so I did. I waited on him to come back any moment, but he never did."

"What did they say? What happened to him?"

"It didn't seem like they knew exactly. He was found drown in the bayou. I guess," she shrugs.

"Weird."

"Yea, I'm kind of freaked out. He's dead. It's bizarre."

"Nothing to be freaked out about, really. Unless you had something to do with his murder."

Her face contorts, appalled I would even suggest such a thing. She hadn't even said *murder.*

"Of course you didn't," I laugh off my statement.

"Madison, did you contact him?" she asks.

"No," I shake my head. "Why would I have?"

"The police showed me some text messages."

My eyes start to cross, *focus, Madison*.

"Texts?" I question.

"Yea, from the old text message app we used at the beginning. The texts were asking to meet him. I don't remember the number, but they look like they are from me. I didn't send those messages. Did you?"

"Wh...what?" I stammer. "No. That's so weird. How would that even happen?"

"They said he was at a bar the night he went into the bayou. The one the text asked to meet him at."

"Hmm."

"Yea, it's very strange. How would anyone text him from that number? If it wasn't me and it wasn't you?"

Shit, shit.

"I don't know. Maybe they recycle numbers after we delete them? And it was some other woman texting from the same number," I shrug.

"That doesn't really make sense, but actually..." She pauses. "Honestly, another woman does make sense with how Tony was."

As confused as she is, she doesn't keep pressing. "I just feel bad. I mean, he was terrible and abused me and others I'm sure. But I mean, I didn't want him dead."

Tony was a terrible person, he hurt so many people, he should have been locked up—now he is dead, now he can't hurt anyone else. No one should feel bad for him.

"Did the cops press you? Do they think you had anything to do with it?" I finally ask.

She shakes her head. "I don't think so. Besides those texts, they didn't seem to have much. They asked how we met and our relationship. They went through my phone. I gave them photos of the abuse and they had me file a report." She takes a breath.

"Where were you the night he died? What night was that? Did they tell you?"

"Yea, the same night you told me to block him. I was with my sister. They called her and she verified. They seemed to take her word."

The cops don't think she had anything to do with it—they would have pressed her further if they did. Does that mean they have their sights on someone else?

"Did you tell them you met him through me?"

"Oh no, I just said the dating app. Essentially, that's how we met."

Thank god she didn't mention my name. We end the call with a goodbye and an empty promise to stay in touch.

THE CONTENTS OF MY desk fits into a small box with room for more.

"Say it isn't so!?!" Robbie cries at my desk.

"I'm sorry, well not sorry." I told my boss this morning, that today was my last day. I know I should have given a two week notice, but I just couldn't continue on. The exhaustion and brain fog I feel every day has made it near impossible to get any work done. At this point, they were just paying me to just sit there—which sounds nice, but it's not right and still takes everything out of me.

"What are you going to do now?" Robbie and Lauri can clearly see something is wrong with me, but I never told them exactly what was happening.

"I'm going to go a little traveling and figure it out."

"That sounds so nice," Lauri says. She wouldn't be envious if she knew the truth.

"One last lunch?" Robbie asks.

It's only 10 in the morning, but I've already turned in my computer.

"I don't think so."

Both Lauri and Robbie look sad but don't say anything more.

"I want to say thank you both for everything. I've had a great time working here with both of you. You both have been so great to me, especially when I wasn't always so great to you." I don't want to cry, but saying goodbye is tougher than I imagined.

"Don't" Tears form in the corner of Robbie's eyes. "We love you so much, Madison." Lauri nods in agreement, forcing a hug on me.

I tried to promise I would pop in for lunch from time to time, but that will be impossible.

"WHO ARE YOU?" TRAVIS spits out.

"Don't worry about it." I hit him with the bat again.

Why did I bring a bat this time? Maybe because I read Travis beat the mother of his child with a bat wrapped in barbed wire. Why did he do that? It doesn't matter, but she had found out he was cheating on her and she confronted him about it.

She was in medical induced coma. He was arrested but was let go on some legal technicalities. He didn't spend more than one night in jail.

Maybe that's why I brought the bat—maybe it's for added protection. Travis seems to be the most violent of the men I've dragged to a bayou.

Travis spits blood and tries to stand. Finally, the drugs have taken effect and he falls back to the ground.

"Travis, Travis, Travis. You had no idea what you were doing signing up to go on a date with the gorgeous Nicole. You are no where good enough for her. She would never."

He looks at me confused. Nicole was the next direct message I had after Rae's message. I didn't want to keep doing this. Once Rae said to delete her profile, I deleted the whole application. Then I got back on TikTok. I intended to delete that too, but I made the mistake of going through my direct messages.

Hi, Madison. I'm Nicole. I've had a few bad experiences with men throughout the years. Physical abuse, emotional abuse, sexual abuse. I recently started dating again and it seems the only way to meet people is on the apps and I just cannot scroll anymore. I would LOVE your help. There's got to be a few good men out there that are emotionally intelligent, mature, and ready to share a life with someone. Let me know if you will help me!

I only meant to offer some encouraging words; but then I offered my services. The message was sent before I could think twice about it. I met Nicole at a coffee shop in the city.

"I don't really drink," she had told me and I told her I didn't either, so she suggested coffee.

"This is soothing my soul," she says as she takes a big gulp. I close my eyes as I sip on my tea—they want to stay shut; I've been so tired lately.

"It's good, huh?" She thinks I'm just enjoying my drink.

"Yup," I lie. "Thanks for meeting me in person."

"No, thank you for meeting me! You are so amazing. I am so surprised you've been able to help so many women in such a short amount of time."

"I mean, honestly, they've been helping themselves. I only found one a man. But they have been able to find and discover themselves. Really figure out what they want out of life."

"So, what you are probably saying is, I probably just need therapy?"

"Don't we all?" We laugh.

"I know I don't need a man. I just am at a point in life where I want a partner to learn and grow with."

"I understand. Tell me more about yourself." I sigh. "That prompt was annoying. I know."

She laughs it off. "Oh, it's okay. I know you are just trying to get to know me better, so you can help me."

"Yea," I say and drink more tea while opening my notebook.

Nicole tells me how she moved to Houston on her own after getting her associates degree. She finished her bachelor's degree at the University of Houston. She enthusiastically tells me how she is working towards owning her own coffee shop one day. Right now she is getting her Master's in

Business Administration and drinking all the coffee around town—market research, she says.

"I love my current job that allows me freedom to pursue my ultimate dreams. I have a great place to live and a wonderful group of friends."

"Is your family here?"

"No, they are back in Florida."

She spends the next 30 minutes explaining the type of relationship she is looking for. She never once describe any physical attributes of the man she pictures herself with, only the things he can add to her life and the things she can add to his.

"Oh my gosh. I just have been talking about myself and my needs the whole time."

"Girl, that is exactly what we are here for! I need to know about you and things you are looking for so I can help!"

"Do you think you can help me?"

"Nicole, can I be completely honest with you?" She nods her head. "I don't know if I can. I don't know if the apps are really what you need."

The air left her in a half-sigh, half-giggle. "I think you're probably right."

"Then, why try this, this way now?"

"I just am so busy. I don't have time to meet anyone in the wild right now."

"That's understandable."

I explain the fee structure and offer her a discount and only a one month contract. She declines; saying she will pay full price for as many months as it takes. She signs the agreement Ellie typed up for me and sent me the money for the first month.

When I got home that night, I created Nicole's profile and it immediately got a ton of attention—like I thought it would. Most of the men who messaged her didn't message back. All but two: Marcus and Travis.

Marcus, a nearly 30-year-old, owns his own home, his own business, adventurous, ready for a relationship, wants kids. Within our first conversation, I deduce he has most, if not all of the qualities, Nicole is looking for in a partner. I message him for a few days, asking a lot of tough questions.

When I posted him on Facebook, I got a lot of women saying how attractive he is and good luck. There was not one negative message about him. However, one woman speculated he might be a catfish. I ran all his information on several different sites and found no criminal records or anything alarming. I also found no evidence he is a catfish.

I passed his information onto Nicole, suggesting a video call to kick things off—she agreed and we set it up immediately. While Nicole and Marcus were having their video call, I researched Travis.

The Facebook post on Travis got almost 250 comments—the most any of my posts have gotten before. This one is a real piece of work. Many of the comments were vague, like "stay away!"—those aren't helpful. However, some were very detailed and informative.

Daisy: I have a child by this man. He abandoned us when I was pregnant after trying to beat the baby out of me.
Kayla: This man manipulated me, lied, somehow got money from my account which he didn't have access.
Marie: I worked with Travis for a few months. He's terrible. Would make such inappropriate comments toward all the women. Bragged about anyone he was sleeping with. Even bragged about trying to beat the baby out of some woman. Cops showed up and arrested him, not sure what for but I never saw him again.

They went on and on, two women asked me to message them privately. I wish I could erase from my mind all the images one sent me.

> I was married to Travis. For about
> five or so years. Things were great

in the beginning, I recognize that
was gaslighting and love bombing.
We moved quickly and I started living with him about 3 months in.
Shortly after, he started the verbal
abuse. He yelled and screamed if
he thought I done anything wrong
or if he thought I looked at another man in a sexual fantasy type way
(later to find out he was out sleeping with multiple women.) One day
brought home HIV to me. When I confronted him, the physical abuse started. I sound stupid for still marry-
ing him after all that, but he convinced me that I wasn't worth anything, I was damaged, and shouldn't
even be alive. After we got married,
we did try for kids, I struggled to con-
ceive. Once I did, he stopped the hitting and I thought things would actually change. Then I miscarried. He
beat me with a bat wrapped in barbed
wire. As I clung to life in the hospital,
he partied and brought women to the
house we shared. I was able to get the
strength and courage to leave with
the help of the friends he once made
me push away. The police tried pur-

suing changes, as did I. Both criminal and civil. But for some reason nothing happened. DV charges are pending, but he has yet to face any actual consequences to what he did to me. I'm sure there's someone else out there with a similar story. Here's some pictures of what he did to me. Please stay away from him.

The second message, from a Brittney, was almost identical without the actual marriage and miscarriage part. However, he also beat this woman with a bat wrapped in barbed wire almost to death.

I messaged the woman who said she had a baby with Travis. Her story echoed the other women's stories. He left her while pregnant, but came back when she had the baby. He beat her with the same bat as well when she refused to have sex with him right after birth. That is when he left for good and has not been in either her or the baby's life since. She said he's not listed on the birth certificate and hope her child never knows or sees him.

What would poses such evil? And why is he allowed to walk this earth doing this to people?

I image the woman lying in the hospital bed, hooked up to every machine, bloody bandages covering her whole body including her face as I unleash another blow to Travis's torso. He cries out in pain.

"Doesn't feel so good, does it?" I taunt him. "Now you know what Brittney and Chelsie felt, huh?"

He doesn't respond and I pull the bat up over my head. As I bring it down on his skull, he screams, quickly moving his hands from his stomach to his bloody scalp. I watch him whither in pain.

"What's going on here?" A panicked man appears on the path along the bayou.

I freeze only momentarily. I have thought about this exact thing happening many times. Fight, flight, or freeze—*what are you going to do, Madison?*

"I don't know," I cry, turning the bat over in my hand. "I just found him and this." I try to hand the bat to the man, but he puts his hands up, refusing to take it.

"Are you okay, sir?" He bends down to check on Travis. "Have you called 9-1-1?" He looks up at me.

"No, I don't have my phone on me." I don't lie. I sound panicked and just as freaked out as him. Quickly, he pulls out his phone to dial 9-1-1.

"Her," Travis tries to talk.

"Shhhh. Help will be here soon. Don't panic, don't worry."

The man walks slightly away to tell the 9-1-1 operator exactly where we are. Once he tells them how to locate us, they stay on the line while he tries to stop some of Travis's bleeding.

Looking back up at me, he says, "Well, help me here."

I don't say a word, I drop the bat in a way so it can roll right off the side of the bayou. It hits the water with a small splash.

"What the. Why did you do that? That's a weapon. Evidence."

I put on my best pity, I'm freaking out face. "I'm sorry, I can't, this." All color vanishes from my face. I start to back away from the scene, I am no longer acting—I might actually get sick.

I hear the ambulance, police, and fire trucks arriving. I have to get out of here before any of them see me. Travis starts moaning in pain again, so the man turns back to focus on him.

This is your chance, Madison. I keep walking backward until there is a bend in the bayou and I can no longer see what is happening with Travis. I turn, taking off in a slight jog, I can't manage much more than that. Once up at the top of the street, my throat burns, body revolting before I can stop it.

Detective Oliver

Jamal from the Twist and Tonic Bar sent over footage from the night. The video clearly shows Madison entering the bar alone and leaving with Travis. The footage inside the bar shows Madison talking with someone sitting at the bar, however, the person is just outside camera shot.

Aida spoke with a bartender working that night—she confirmed seeing Madison with Travis. She also said she looks like the woman who was with Matthew. When we spoke with her initially, she couldn't confirm it was Madison, but seeing her the second night, she is sure they are the same and that it is Madison.

Liam knocks on my door. "Hey Oliver."

"Hey, Liam." He comes only a few steps into my office.

"Gabriel is here."

I stand. "Oh, great."

We head to the conference room. "Liam," I say. "Why don't you take the lead on this one?"

"Sure." He smiles and I know letting him lead the interview means a lot to him.

Liam introduces us as we enter the room. We sit across from the man who witnessed the crime against Travis.

"Gabriel, can you tell us what happened that night?" Liam starts.

"Is that man okay?" Gabriel asks before answering Liam's question.

"He's in critical condition, but we hope he will be okay." I say.

"Can you start from the beginning? Why were you on the Brays Bayou that day?"

"I was just taking a walk. Wait a minute. Am I a suspect?" Panic sets in.

"No, sir. We just want to get the full picture of what happened."

He takes a breath. "I was just out for a walk."

"Do you normally walk along the bayou at night?" Liam asks.

Gabriel shakes his head. "No, I just moved over to this side of town. Thought I would check it out. This was only my second evening out there."

"Did you notice anything unusual the other time?"

"Nope, I wouldn't have been out there if I had. I won't ever go out there again."

"Okay, so you were out for a walk? And?" Liam prompts Gabriel to keep going.

"Yea, so I was out for a walk. Had gotten about a mile in when I heard a man and woman. They were talking but it didn't sound friendly."

"At the time you heard them, could you see them?"

He shakes his head. "No, the bayou had a curve in it, so I could only hear them. Then it sounded like something hit something. I didn't know but I guess it was the bat hitting the man." He winces as if he is being hit.

No one says anything for a few moments. Liam wants to fill the silence, add in commentary, ask another question. He resists the urge, letting Gabriel finally start talking again.

"When I went around the bend, I saw the man curled up on the ground, bleeding. And a woman, standing over him. She had a bat. I startled her." He gulps, but his mouth is dry. He's clearly shook up over the whole situation.

I grab him a bottle of water from the side table in the room. He opens it and downs half of it in a few gulps. Using the back of his hand he wipes the water off his chin, like he is a small child.

"She said she had just walked up on the man as well. But I was skeptical. I bent down to check on the man immediately. He couldn't really speak, he was bleeding profusely. The woman said she didn't have her phone on her, so I also called 9-1-1. The woman just stood there, doing nothing. Finally she dropped the bat, it rolled into the water and then she ran away."

"Can you describe the woman?" Liam asks.

Gabriel described Madison. From her hair color, to the entire outfit she wore that night as recorded on the security footage, including the types of shoes she was wearing. Liam looks at me—I know he is thinking that we for sure have enough on Madison. However, with what we have and one eye witness, still isn't enough. Not to mention, we can't find her at the moment.

"Do you think that woman hurt that man?" Gabriel asks.

"We can't discuss an active investigation." I state.

Gabriel nods his head in understanding. I stand to start to leave—Liam can wrap up this interview and fill me in on anything important later.

"Gabriel, thank you so much for coming in today." I say as I exit. Liam nods to me exiting.

"Hey, baby mama." James says as I climb into his car.

We laugh and I say, "Probably shouldn't call me that."

"Okay," James keeps laughing as he drives us to our doctor's appointment.

Before we head up to see the doctor, we stop at the sonogram office. We walk right in the room to get started—thankfully I am far enough a long that we can do an abdominal sonogram and I don't have to get undressed.

"Jelly is going to be cold," the sonographer says as she is smearing it all over my swollen belly.

James stands next to me, holding my hand, as the image of our baby fills the television screen on the wall.

Blurb, blurb. The sound of her tiny, fast heart beat fill the room. Tears form at the edge of my eyes.

The sonographer takes measurements—whatever that means—and prints out a few pictures for us to take with us. Growing a baby inside my body is extraordinary, and being able to see her growth month to month is just incredible. Honestly, I wish I could see her, hear her heart beat, make sure she is doing well every day, not just every few weeks.

"I'm really worried about you." James says as we sit in the waiting room in the doctor's office. I look at him confused. "Your job is so stressful. I don't want anything bad to happen."

I peel his hand off my stomach. *Does he blame me and my job for our struggle in getting pregnant? Is it my fault we struggled all those years?*

James puts his arms back around me. "Please don't take that the wrong way. Of course I don't want anything happening to the baby, but I don't want anything happening to you either. You are my number one priority."

"If you had to choose, something terrible happened and the doctor has you pick between saving my life or the baby's life. Which do you pick?"

"You." He answers before I can even finish my question. "Like I hope it never comes to that. But you. You every day."

I wonder, did I want him to pick me? Or did I want him to save our innocent baby's life—one that wouldn't get a chance at life? The nurse calls my name before I can think about it anymore.

The nurse takes my vitals, weight, heart rate, blood pressure, temperature—all normal. After the conversation in the waiting room did have me worried my blood pressure would be high, maybe James has nothing to worry about.

The doctor comes in the room as the nurse is finishing up her notes; something that never happens, normally we are waiting on her to finish up with other patients.

"Tell me how you are feeling." She says as she sits.

I tell her I have been feeling great— a little more tired than normal and of course eating more. She tells me both are normal even for a healthy pregnancy. I glare at James.

"We want to make sure this stays a healthy pregnancy," James chimes in, ignoring my stare. "You know Grace has a highly stressful job for anyone who isn't pregnant."

"James! Detectives have had babies before," I snap. The emotion from the earlier conversation clearly bubbling up.

"Of course. Stress is always something we want to manage and be cautious of, especially when pregnant. However, everything looks great as of now. The baby is growing at the rate she needs to be. You look great, your blood pressure is perfect." The doctor says to me, not James. I shoot James another look.

"Now," the doctor continues. "If any of that changes, let me know and we can address that then."

We wrap up the appointment with the doctor and leave the office in silence. James drives me back to work.

"I understand why you are worried." I say. "If anything happens to her," I put my hand on my belly. "I will never forgive myself. But we have to trust everything is going to be okay. I promise to pay attention to my body and if I feel like anything is wrong, I'll let you know."

He nods, kisses me, and I get out of the car. I finally let out a breath.

Liam is in my office when I get back from the doctor.

"Sorry, I was waiting on you. Didn't know where to wait." Liam says. I shrug him off.

I set all of my stuff back in it's place in my office. Before I put my purse away, I take a sonogram picture out and pin it to my bulletin board.

"Oh, I didn't know you were at a doctor's appointment." Liam stands to examine the picture I put up. "Crazy that is inside you."

I laugh so loud, I almost snort. "Well that's one way to put it."

"I just mean..."

"I know, it is pretty crazy." I continue laughing as I sit at my desk.

"We called Madison's dad again. I don't understand why we can't go out there to him. Why were we able to go to Kentucky but can't go to Utah?"

He shakes it off before I can answer—not that I have an answer.

"He told us something interesting."

"Oh?" I ask, impatiently.

"He says Madison killed her cousin. The one Ellie said died when she was in college and seemed happier after he died."

Trying to put the pieces together, since Liam is dragging out the details, as always; I ask "Madison killed her cousin?"

"That's what he said." Liam shrugs.

"Well, what else did he say? Why did she kill him? How does he know for sure it was her? What happened? How did she kill him?"

"He said he helped her cover it up."

"Liam!" I almost yell. "Tell me everything right now! What all did he say?!"

Liam apologizes for being so cryptic and then spills everything. According to Madison's father, she claimed her cousin was sexually assaulting her for years—he didn't believe his nephew could do such a thing, especially since they grew up like siblings. Madison went home during a break from school and he tried to assault her again and she didn't just fight back, she shot him in the face. He bled out on her childhood bed, the scene of most of the abuse. Madison's father helped her stage it as a suicide.

"Did he just offer up all this information?"

"He did. He seemed really angry at Madison. He's been trying to call her, but she hasn't been answering. He says she hasn't visited since she killed her cousin."

"Was there an investigation?" I ask.

Liam shakes his head. "I guess the dad is cool with some of the cops, he asked them to respect how hard this was on the family, they cremated the body quickly. Buried all evidence."

"So basically, it's just hearsay. We don't really know what happened?"

"Yea. But it tracks if she really is our killer."

Liam is right. A man doing awful things seems to be Madison's modus operandi. This might have been the reason she believes she can continue to bring this vigilante type justice.

"Ellie! It's Detective Oliver and Detective Callahan. Thank you so much getting back to us so quickly." I say hastily.

Liam and I called Ellie a few hours ago—it went straight to voicemail, we asked her to call us back, but I wasn't going to hold my breath waiting. I didn't think she would, as it seems she is very protective of her friend.

"Of course. Have you found Madison?" She still sounds worried.

"No, we haven't. Have you heard from her?"

"No." Something in her voice tells me, she is lying.

"We were wondering if you could tell us any more about her cousin that died." I say, unsure of how to ask a question about him.

"I don't really know much."

"Do you know if he was harming her in any way?"

She gasps. "That's who it was."

"Who what was, Ellie?"

"There was one night, I think Madison had drank way too much. She normally didn't drink because of the meds she had to take, but that night she had a few too many. It was during the whole hashtag metoo movement. She mentioned she could use that hashtag. I asked her about it, she just said that it was a long time ago and it was over. Maybe it was her cousin? Maybe that's why she seemed happier after he died? Because he couldn't hurt her anymore." She is making real-time connections.

"Did she say how he died?"

"He shot himself." She takes a deep breath and let's it out into the phone.

"We think she might have had something to do with his death." I test the waters.

"Really?" She doesn't sound too surprised.

"We think she might be involved in hurting other men too. It's very important, if you hear from her, you contact us immediately."

"Of course." I don't believe her. "I've known Madison a long time and I'm not sure she would hurt anyone."

"I understand. We just need to talk to her to make sure." I'm about to end the conversation when I pause.

"Hey, did you get a hold of Kevin? He might know where she is."

"Ellie, Kevin doesn't exist."

"What do you mean he doesn't exist?" Her voice trembles with genuine shock.

"We cannot find any evidence Madison was dating anyone or even knew anyone named Kevin."

"Are you sure?" Ellie realizes she might not know her friend as well as she thought.

We are sure. As strange as it seems, Madison made up a boyfriend. Through many legal channels, we were able to gain access to Madison's phone records including any activity she had on her phone including all applications that were downloaded. Madison never had any contact with anyone named Kevin, or any man other than the ones she either killed or set up with other women.

I thank Ellie for her cooperation and reiterate the importance of contacting me if Madison reaches out to her. She says she understands, but I still don't believe she will.

Madison

WHAT THE FUCK ARE you doing, Madison?

I ditched the clothes I was wearing while trying to kill Travis in dumpsters along the drive home. Just hoping there was no cameras—I tried to pick old, sketchy looking places for dumpsters. I also drove the loop, outside the loop, south side, north side dumping them in various places. Criminals get caught because they leave obvious evidence, *right?*

I have no idea how to be a criminal. I never even stolen anything. Yet, somehow I am a living, breathing criminal.

I let the phone ring multiple times, but if I don't want to pick up, Ellie will be concerned and keep calling until I do answer.

"Hey, Ellie."

"Oh!" She seems shocked. "Madison, are you okay?"

I shake my head. "I'm really not feeling well."

"You don't look well."

"Thanks, Ellie," I try to laugh it off.

"Not like that!" She tries to back track. I wave her off.

"Madison, why is a detective asking me questions? And why did you change your number? I've been so terribly worried and not been able to get a hold of you!"

I texted Ellie a few days that I lost my phone—of course, a lie. I threw it out along the path, throwing out my clothes that night.

I lose my breath. If I didn't just throw up, I would be vomiting right now.

"Who? What?" I try to sound calm, as if the detective has no business interrogating Ellie.

"Yea. A Detective Oliver asked me a bunch of questions about you."

"Like what?"

"She asked about how we know each other, your past, stuff like that. It was weird, she asked if you were a violent person."

"What did you tell her?"

Ellie laughs, nervously. "I told her no, of course. But why would she even think you were?"

I can't bring myself to answer.

"She said they were investigating something and they seemed to have a connection to you. She wouldn't tell me what exactly though."

"What?" I let out a laugh. "How is that even possible?"

Fuck, Madison.

"Does this have to do with the ghost dating?"

"Huh? I don't even meet those men. The women do. Wait, did she say something was happening to men?"

"No, she wouldn't give specific details of the case. But I did look up some stuff and it does look like there's been a few men turn up dead in the bayou out there?"

"God, that's awful. I haven't heard about that."

Fuck, what am I going to do now?

"Really? Is it safe for you there?"

"If she calls again, let me know. I wonder why no one has reached out to me? Like why call you before they come to me?"

"I don't know, Madison. It really scared me, though."

"I bet. I'm so sorry, Ellie." She should have never been dragged into this.

"Is there anything you need to tell me?" She asks.

"No."

I look away from the screen and her concerned face. This is who I am now—I lie to my best friend and I murder men. What a way to end my life.

"Madison, I am also concerned for your health." She sounds like a broken record now.

"Please, stop worrying about me. I know it's scary for you, but it isn't for me. It's the end and I've accepted it."

She starts to cry and I feel bad for her. I have had so many years to face my own mortality; while she was there for some of it too, she always had hope the disease would leave my body and I'd live a normal long life. I knew that was never a possibility. Maybe it was all those years when I was younger wishing I was dead; it's finally happening, years too late.

"Ellie, please don't cry. It's all going to be okay. You're going to be okay. And one day, soon, I won't be in any more pain."

Between sobs, I assume she tries to tell me how much she loves me and will miss me.

Nick appears on the screen. "Madison, I'm sorry again. We love you. Ellie, this stress isn't good for the baby."

We say bye and he promises to have Ellie call me back soon. Shortly, after we hand up, Ellie texts she is sorry. Sorry for what? I'm not sure. But all Ellie has ever done is love me in a way no one else has.

My thoughts float from Ellie to this detective. *What am I doing to do about that?* I have been so careful, *how did they even make that connection?*

THE GUN SHOT STILL echoes in my brain. Not a shot heard around the world, but one that changed the course of my life forever.

"What the fuck have you done?" My dad yells two inches from my face.

My feet glued to the carpet, my eyes crossed, my breath shallow.

"Snap out of it, Madison," my dad shakes me before loosening my grip on the gun. He unloads the firearm, setting it on the dresser.

How did the gun get in my hand? How long have I been standing here, paralyzed, while my cousin bleeds out on my bed?

"He," I choke out.

"Don't start, Madison. Don't start claiming he was trying to attack you again."

"He was. Again. He has been. All these years." I start retreating into myself, tears fall.

"Emmett would never. And now look what you have gone and done. Get out of here, I'll handle this."

I have no idea what he is going to do to handle "this," but I run. I run and I never go back.

Man Attacked at Brays Bayou

Top news headline reads when I open up the application. I can only read a few paragraphs of the article because I haven't paid the subscription fee for full access. What I could read said a man was found by a civilian badly beaten on the walking path along the Brays Bayou. The man is in critical condition—he's in a coma at a local hospital. The article praises the civilian for saving the man's life. Neither men is named. Again, from the small snippet, there's no mention of a female civilian or suspects or a bat. I consider paying the fee, but since I quit my job, I don't have much extra funds to waste on things like this.

Anyway, this is the last time any of this happens. I am done ghost dating; I am done murdering. I've got the last bits out of my apartment. I'll be long gone before the detective really gets to me—well, that's what I am hoping for. The doctor says it's not much longer and if it is, maybe I'll head to Oregon. I heard they have a good end of life care there.

Detective Oliver

Madison posted a video—brave of her to continue to post. At this point, I'm sure her friend has made it clear we are onto her. The video is her goodbye, she is shutting down her account, she is done ghost dating. Madison looks ill, like her body is shutting down on her.

I basically run out of my office to Liam's desk. "Liam!"

Liam, surprised to see me move so fast, says "Um, you okay?"

"No. Yes. I've got an idea. Where's Aida?" I say looking around for her.

"I'm not sure?" He says it likes it's a question, but I think he is just questioning my lunacy.

"Find her and meet me in the conference room."

I am writing on the white board when Aida and Liam join me.

"What's up, Oliver? You seem frantic." Liam says.

"I am. No, I'm not. But we have to find Madison fast." I say.

"And you have an idea on how we can do that?"

Liam sits at the table, Aida continues to stand waiting to hear me out.

"Yes! Clearly what does Madison hate?" I look to them to answer, they don't. "She hates men who mistreats women."

They both nod along; I am not telling them anything they don't already know.

"How much coffee had you had today?" Liam asks. I don't think I've ever been this excited before. "Isn't coffee bad for the baby?" His hand covers his mouth as fast as it can, but he can't shove the words back in.

"Baby?!" Aida questions. "You're pregnant?" Her face lights up.

I nod and rub my belly—I won't be able to hid it much longer, anyway.

"Congrats!!" She runs to my side of the table, pulling me into a hug.

"Thanks! And I have only had one cup." I roll my eyes—Liam should know better than to comment on what someone does with their body, especially one growing a human life.

"I just think. What if we, if you," I point to Liam, "pose as a man who has done horrible things to women. We'll essentially lure her out thinking she is going to 'kill' off another bad man." I put kill in air quotes.

"You want to catfish her, make her think she is going out to kill me, and then, what?"

"We will arrest her," I say, waiting on them to affirm this is the most brilliant idea they have ever heard.

"Okay," Aida starts. "How do we do that though? She doesn't date for herself. She ghost dates for other people."

"Yes! That's where you come in, Aida. You will pose as a woman who desperately needs help finding a man. She won't be able to resist trying to help you, we'll set up Liam a profile on the dating app for her to find. You'll have to be as vulgar as possible so she'll want to take you out."

I nearly laugh—all of it—this whole ordeal is laughable. There's a woman out there, who, it seems, just wanted to help other women find decent men to date, and instead she has been murdering them.

"We will have to set up dating profiles, create a criminal history for Liam, even create Facebook profiles to comment on her posts, since she heavily relies on the stories of other women," Aida says.

"Yes, I've started making a list." I point to the white board.

"Now that makes more sense," Liam says. "You think this could work? Didn't she just post she was giving up the ghost dating?"

"She did. But she hasn't deleted the app just yet. We have to create a woman's profile and back story quickly. We need to get her attention fast!"

We spend about ten minutes brainstorming a profile for a woman named Lyn. Lyn is desperate to find a man, she loves to read, run, and photography. She is essentially Aida with a different name and just the type of woman Madison would want to help.

"We need her whole profile ready," Liam says. "What should Lyn do?"

"A teacher. I always wanted to be a teacher," Aida says.

This surprises me, however, I could see Aida teaching some new officer or new detective classes in the future. Or even at the collegiate level for those wanting to enter the criminal justice field. I mentally file that away to bring up to her in the future. But first we have a serial killer to catch.

"Sounds great. You think you can put together a profile for the man Liam will play?" I ask.

They nod and start getting to work. I head to tell the captain our plan.

The conference room phone's cry cut through the quiet, startling us into motion. Liam made it to the phone first.

"Detectives," the woman on the other end of the phone says. "I've got a Doctor Marie Morgan on the line."

"Put her through. Thank you," Liam says, as I move closer to the phone.

"Doctor Morgan, hello, this is Detective Oliver and Detective Callahan."

"Yes, I'm sorry I wasn't in when you guys where down at my office. I got your request for Madison Anderson's medical file."

After learning about Madison's illness, finding her doctor didn't take much detective work. However, when we went to the office the doctor was out for the day and we didn't have an actual warrant for the records.

"I am sending over the secure file now," the doctor says.

My inbox pings notifying my the receipt of the file.

"I got it, doctor. Thank you." I open the file, however, I don't understand any of the words.

The doctor reads my confusion through the silence. "Madison has ovarian cancer."

"Is it treatable?"

"Not at this stage. She seemed to have missed a few check up appointments that could have caught it earlier. They should have taken her ovaries when she was younger. She also had a very rare case of ovarian cancer when she was a teen. They did what they thought was best, I guess. But she should have had her ovaries removed to prevent this from happening now." There's a softness woven in her tone; I can hear how much she cares about her patients.

"How long does she have?"

"A few months, maybe just weeks."

"Oh wow." Liam gasps.

"She responded to our message!" Aida's face lit up as soon as I walked back into the conference room.

"She did? Already?"

Honestly, I am a bit surprised. This was my plan, but I was still a little bit skeptical it would actually work. Joe is very skeptical it will work the way I want it to.

Liam nods and shows me the message. Madison bought the sob story we sold her and she asks for a video call to get to know Lyn better.

"Let's get you ready for this call!" I say.

Aida looks nervous, but I know she will do great.

"Is this our first official undercover operation?" Liam asks, excitedly; I nod.

Liam has a good, long detective career ahead of him. If we can pull this off, it will look great for him.

"Show me your dating profile Liam." He pulls up the dating app on the television screen.

"Liam!" I scream and hit his back.

"What?"

"Why did you use your real first name?!"

"Oh shit. I didn't even think about it when I put it in."

"Oh Liam." I almost laugh. "We can't mess this up."

"I promise, that's the only thing I kept the same." He keeps scrolling. "Well, of course the pictures."

"Okay, good. We need to get this right." I glance around the room, sighing. "Aida, schedule the video call as soon as possible. Let's get Madison to put up Lyn's profile and get Liam connecting with her."

Aida nods and I assume she is contacting Madison to schedule the call. Once they make that connection, we can move forward with this plan. Meanwhile, Liam shows me the fake criminal record he set up for himself—when Madison does her research, she will find this and be appalled. She will want to murder him in an instance.

I bound in the house, tossing my bag and shoes at the door. I know James will be annoyed by this, but today, I don't bother with them.

"James!" I call for him in a singsong way as I make my way through the house—finding him in the kitchen, of course.

"You look happy," He says as I kiss him.

"I am so excited!"

"What is it?"

"We are going to get her, James."

"Um." He's confused. "Get who? Her?"

"Madison."

I see he's caught up with me.

"You guys found her?"

"Not yet. I came up with this genius plan to get her out of hiding, or where ever she is." I laugh at myself, calling it a genius plan I came up with.

I quickly explain to him the plan and he assures me it is in fact genius.

Aida texted that Madison had a video call with "Lyn" shortly after I left the station. Liam noticed the dating profile was set up almost immediately. He matched with her and sent her a vulgar message. Madison should not be able to resist it. If she does, we have a few back up profiles we can set up that might entice her.

I keep refreshing the Facebook group, to see if Madison has posted Liam to find out more information on him. Each of us have about five fake women's profiles on Facebook to comment, when she does post.

This is going to work. It has to work. We have to catch this woman that has been murdering men in my city.

Madison

Should I even be posting on TikTok? Probably not, but my account is still getting so much attention; I feel like I owe them a goodbye.

Beep. Beep. Beep.

"Good morning, loves! From the bottom of my heart I want to thank this community. You guys have allowed me to open up, make great connections, help women find themselves. However, due to personal reasons, I am closing this chapter. This account will be shut down in a few days and I will move onto the next thing. Again, thank you all. Love ya!" *#ghostdater*

123.5k views; 68k likes; 891 saves; 525 comments

Comments:

Emilio Sam: Thank god fat bitch.

Ashen Whispers: Nooooooooo!!!

Its.livvy: Ah man. I sent you a message a while back, wishing you could have helped me!

Miaa Starr: Good for you for recognizing you are ready for the next best thing.

Ethan_exe: Get off my screen.

TaylorTrends: Good luck!

Rae24: Thank you for helping me!

Noah Wavers: You didn't anyone. Go away.

Luke+gets+laid: Sad to see you leave, love to watch you go.

Lilzoezoe: You're awesome girl. Loved watching this journey. Will miss seeing your face.

Hey.its.Ryan: Don't delete this account! Keep us updated on your next adventures.

At least the comments have been consistent—for every negative one, there's at least five positive ones. I open the messages one last time.

Message from BradleyBoo:

Youuuuu suck...

Delete.

Message from AmeliaBedilia:

I love what your...

Delete.

Message from Lily34:

Need help...

Delete.

Message from Coach Lane:

> Just stop…

Delete.

Message from Lyn Rose Reads:

> Please don't delete! I need your help. My name is Lyn. I'm from a small town in Texas but been in Houston a while. At one point, I had my whole life planned out down to when I would marry my high school sweetheart and have his babies. I blew up my life by moving away when he didn't want to. I've dated a few men here and there, but not someone I could see myself with for longer than a few months. It's just been rough, but I'm ready to let someone in. Would love your help, please.

Why did I keep reading this particular message? I recognize the username. They recently left comments on all my ghost dater videos. I go back to my comments—the first one from Lyn read "I just found you, so late to the game. I so need your help! Messaged you."

The second comment "Love what you are doing! Hope you get to my message to help me too!" Similar comments on all my videos I have posted about ghost dating. I wonder how she just found my account and then left comments on every video in the last few hours.

I said I was done. This was my goodbye—my last video. Nicole was the last woman I tried helping. Travis was my last victim.

Or...was it? Should I help one more woman? I don't have to hurt anyone else. Just ghost date, as I intended in the first place. I can do that. I can find Lyn her person. And then...then I am done. Then I'll be done with ghost dating for good.

"THANK YOU SO MUCH for reaching out to me! I was so nervous when I saw your goodbye video. I thought you were done?"

Lyn is smiling on the other side of the phone. She donned a light purple cardigan that somehow clashes against her jet black hair. Glass doors appear behind her as if she is in a conference room. I check the time. Well, most people would be a work at this time, not everyone quit at the same time I did.

"I was. Well I am. I think you'll be my last client. I don't think I have the time or the capacity to keep doing this."

"Is everything okay? I appreciate you taking me on!"

"Yea, I'm good. And of course. I hope I can help. Let's get started." I open my notebook, writing 'Lyn' at the top of a clean page.

Before she starts talking about herself and the things she is looking for in a man, I write down some things I already know.

29, teacher living in Houston, from sml town in Texas

"Let's start with what you like to do."

She tells me she is a runner who like photography. Lyn loves to travel and be outside. While it's been challenging to make friends being new to Houston, she has a few friends that get together for book club and brunch.

"Do you have any trips planned?" I ask.

Her face lights up. "Yes! Since summer break from school is coming, I am planning a trip to Spain."

"Oh wow! That sounds amazing." I am genuinely jealous, or is it envy? It's the good kind though—I want her to have the experience, but I want it too.

"Is it a solo trip?"

She pauses a moment, and I wonder if she doesn't want to tell a stranger her travel plans.

"Part of it, yes. One of my friends back home is going to meet me out there for a few days."

"Very cool." I don't press for more details, but can't help myself saying, "I'd love to see pictures, so I can live through you. I always wanted to go to Spain."

She nods. One thing I didn't get a chance to do in this life is travel. I feel like I really missed out on something special.

"Alright, let's get what you are looking for in a partner."

"Six foot, at least." She laughs. "I'm kidding, but isn't that what everyone says these days. Height doesn't really matter to me. I mean, I'm short, so most people are taller than me anyway. Hell, even some of my students are taller than me!"

We both chuckle; height is something that seems to be important to some. Like the taller the man, the better he is?

"No, I am looking for someone who is emotionally mature, who wants a true partner, wants to grow and learn together, travel, and have fun."

I take notes, although these are basic things everyone is looking for in a connection with another human. Again, Lyn doesn't list physical attributes of a person.

She continues. "If we aren't making each other better, what's the point?" Lyn's comment sounds familiar, but I can't place it.

"Oh for sure. I think people get too caught up in the physical aspects or the instant chemistry. It's not sustainable."

"Yea, there definitely needs to be some chemistry though or at least attraction."

"Of course. There just needs to be more than that though," I say and let the silence linger between us.

"Speaking of that, is there any physical attributes you are attracted to or not? You joked about height, but is there anything else?"

She thinks for a minute. "Honestly, I don't think so. I've dated all races, all body types. It was always something personality related that made me end it."

I write down 'no physical type.' Then I ask her to tell me about her last few relationships; she hesitates.

"That's hard to talk about," She finally says.

"You don't have to go into too much detail. Can I just know when it was, how long it lasted and what you learned?"

Lyn swallowed hard. "It was about two years ago and it lasted about three years, I think."

She pauses and I let her collect her thoughts.

"The biggest lesson I learned was to never let anyone try to control me. My ex slowly isolated me from my friends and family. I lost myself."

"I'm sorry. I'm glad you learned that and you should be with someone who elevates you, not isolates you."

"You think I can find someone like that?"

"Of course! And you deserve someone like that."

She beams. I explain how the process works and how much my services cost.

"That's all. Man, I think you are definitely undercharging."

I awkwardly laugh. "Actually, it was more, but you will be my last client, so a little discount feels necessary."

"Ah, why are you quitting?"

"I just think it's time to move on. I'm ready for a change." I don't want to divulge much more, so I leave it at that.

"I understand. What's next?" She asks—the only real answer is death.

I shrug. "Not sure. Maybe a novel. Still trying to really figure it out." I smile, weakly.

"Yes, a novel would be great. A novel about ghost dating? I'm sure you have a ton of stories."

She has no idea the stories I have. Lyn is truly excited and I hate this will be the last time I get to meet another amazing woman.

"I can't believe I will be your last client."

"Yea, definitely a little bittersweet. I'm excited to work with you." I explain I will create her profile and have her send me a variety of pictures to add to it.

We say our goodbyes and the exhaustion hits suddenly. Sitting up and talking that much really takes everything I have—I lay down my car seat and am asleep before I know it.

WHAT'S THAT?! My phone jolts me awake. I clumsily answer it, while dropping it between the seat and console.

"Madison?"

I pick up the phone and Ellie's concerned face fills the screen.

"Hey, Ellie."

"Where you sleeping? Are you in your car?!" She asks, strangely accusatory, as if sleep is wrong, or being in my car is wrong. Maybe sleeping in my car is wrong?

I yawn. "Yea?"

"I'm sorry for waking you, I guess."

"It's fine. What's up?"

"What's going on with you, Madison?"

"Nothing, why?" I say.

I want to say "I'm just here, dying," but I know she won't appreciate the humor in it.

"Madison, the detective called me."

"Again?! What?! Why? What did she say?"

"She was asking if I had heard from you."

"What did you say?"

"I lied. I told her I haven't heard from you. Why are they still looking for you? Maybe you should go talk to them. Clear all this up, whatever it is."

"I can't." A breath slips out, low and tired.

What am I supposed to do, just walk into a police station and tell them I've been the one murdering men? No, I can't do that. I can't spend my last moments on this earth in a jail cell.

"What?" Ellie bursts.

I let the moment hang, unfilled.

"They said Kevin doesn't exist. Why would they say that?" Is that anger I detect in her voice?

"Shit, Ellie." I gather my thoughts. "I didn't want to tell you, but we called off the wedding."

"Don't," she whispers. "They said there was never a Kevin. No person. No engagement. No wedding."

"And you believe the police and not me, your best friend?" I really laid that one on and immediately regret it.

"Honestly, I'm not really sure what I believe anymore." She sighs, heavily.

"Well, I don't know where they got their information from. How would they even know?"

"I don't know, because they are the police? They have resources."

"Whatever." I roll my eyes. "We broke up. I'm dying. That's all."

"So, Kevin was *so* great and you wanted to marry him, but he just left you when you were dying?" I think that is the first time Ellie has let herself say it out loud: that I'm running out of time.

"Yup. He wasn't so great after all." I let my eyes escape upward, anywhere but here. "The last few months ghost dating have really taught me men are shit."

"I saw your video. You're also quitting that?"

"I can't do it anymore. It's all too exhausting." I think that's the only thing she believes.

"I'm glad you are going to take a break from it, then."

"It's not a break, Ellie. It's over. It's all over for me."

Detective Oliver

The sterile smell reminds me I haven't been in a hospital in years. I walked these same halls, correction, I ran these halls after my dad had a heart attack, many years ago. Terrified I would lose him before I could say goodbye, I rushed to him. He had surgery and changed his lifestyle completely—thankfully, he made a full recovery and is doing better than ever. He even ran a marathon a few months back.

"Thank you," Liam says to the nurse that led us to Travis's room.

Travis tries sitting up in his bed. He can't quite do it himself, wincing in pain. Bloody gauze is wrapped tightly around his head.

"Please don't try to get up, Travis." Liam tells him as we enter the room. Travis gives up and slumps back down in defeat.

Liam introduces us. "We want to get your account of what happened the night you were attacked."

Travis stays silence.

"Can you tell us who attacked you?" I ask.

Travis doesn't even look at me.

"Travis?"

"I don't want to talk to a bunch of cops." He finally says, staring at the wall in front of him. "I told them to keep all of you out of my room!"

"Travis, we want to capture the person who did this to you. We don't want them to do this to anyone else. And we want them to pay for doing this to you," Liam says.

Travis moves and cries out in pain. He presses the button on his bed calling for a nurse.

"Do you know who attacked you?"

Travis shakes his head.

"Was it a male?"

He shakes his head.

"So a female?"

He nods.

"Can you describe her?"

Silence. *What is happening here? Why is Travis not telling us who attacked him?*

A nurse comes in the room. "What do you need, Travis?" She says curtly, her bedside manner leaves a lot to be desired.

"I'm in pain." He doesn't look at her either and now I understand why she was being so short with him. She gives me a weak understanding smile.

She checks something and then tells him he can't have any more pain medicine yet. Travis tries throwing the television remote he had clutched in his right hand. It frustrates him more that the remote is connected to the bed. Without the satisfaction of breaking plastic against the wall, he slumps further down.

"I'm really confused," I try to sound empathetic, but it's a weak try. "Don't you want to help us get this person that put you here?"

"Listen," His voice is low and deep. "Some bitch drugged me, led me down to the bayou and beat the shit out of me. I should have killed her, but I didn't. I couldn't. I just laid there like a little bitch."

Suddenly, I understand. He's embarrassed, he's a strong man that couldn't fight someone—a female—off of him. This time, he wasn't the dominate one calling the shots, or taking the shots.

"Travis, do you think you could identify the person who attacked you from a lineup?" I don't say female, hoping to not bruise his ego any more than it is and hope he will cooperate.

However, he doesn't say anything. We aren't getting any-thing else out of him at this point.

"What the fuck?" I say a little too loud in the hallway.

Liam laughs at my uncharacteristic outburst and we walk out of the hospital in silence.

"Detective?" Aida jolts me out of my thoughts.

"Sorry." I shake it off. She points to Liam.

"I just got a message from Madison."

I wonder how long they were trying to get my atten-tion—I was lost thinking about what would happen if this didn't work out. What if we can't catch the Ghost Dater? It looks like, I might not have to find out.

"Well...what's it say?" I ask, eagerly.

He scrunches his face. "She wants to meet at the bayou. She suggested meeting at a small park and talking a walk?"

I mimic his face in the same confusion. This isn't her normal meeting place, sure the bayou, but typically she takes men to a bar first. *What is she planning with Liam? Maybe she isn't going to try to kill him?*

"What do we do?" Aida asks.

"We have to agree. We got to meet her where she wants."

"Done." Liam sets his phone down triumphantly.

"What did you message her?" Aida wants to know all the details, keep all of the facts straight.

"That I will meet her."

"Okay? But when? And what's the actual location?"

"Tomorrow at 7:30." Mine and Aida's phone ping; he's forwarded the location of the park.

"We need to plan this out. So we are in charge."

"What do you mean?" Liam asks. "Can't we arrest her as soon as she pulls up to the park?"

"No, Liam. Unfortunately, we can't."

I stand heading to the dry erase board. I erase it's contents drawing the Brays Bayou in it's place. In red I circle the park.

"Liam, you will meet Madison here."

I grab the green marker. I draw a line down the bayou and circle another area.

"We will be here. You will need to take a walk with Madison. See if she will give up any information or if she attempts to take your life."

A breathless burst of laughter escapes Liam. "So I just wait to see if she kills me?"

"Liam, you will be armed. Aida and I will be there with more officers. She won't kill you. And you know how to swim, right?" A mischievous grin sneaks out.

"Nothing is going to happen to you, Liam. I promise. We just need to catch her in her attempt."

He nods. "I understand. I will be fine. And I know you won't let anything bad happen to me."

"You just have to get her walking and talking." I glance back down at some notes. "Oh, were we able to get a location from her call with you, Aida?" She shakes her head.

Madison

MESSAGE FROM JUAN:

> **Show me those titties!**

That's the first message I open from the dating application after setting up Lyn's profile. I let out an audible sigh—*what's wrong with people?* I delete the message and move onto the next one.

Message from Mike:

> **Hello, you're pretty.**

> **Hi! Thank you.**

> **You're welcome.**

That seemed to be the end of that conversation.

Message from Jeffery:

> **You are literally conquer the whole world with that beautiful smile.**

> That's a beautiful compliment. Thank you.

Message from Liam:

> You look like you can suck it good.

What the actual fuck? Do these guys think they really can get away with this stuff?

Message from Jamie:

> Hello, Lyn. I noticed you love photography and traveling. That's an awesome combo. What has been your favorite place you've been and been able to take photos from?

> Hi James! The best place I've been so far for both has been Hawaii.

> I was wondering if that photo on your profile was in Hawaii. I'd love to see more pictures on day. I'd also love to visit it myself one day.

Clapping in my head for Jamie; way to pay attention to the profile and carry on a good conversation. Am I celebrating a man doing the bare minimum? But I am glad I also asked Lyn the same question when she sent over the pictures.

> Seeing it in person is definitely a must! Jamie, do you travel much?

While waiting on Jamie to respond, I delete five more disgusting messages suggesting they only want one thing from Lyn.

"GOOD MORNING, ELLIE."

I forgot Ellie and I scheduled a call for this morning. We have made it to the age where we have to make sure time is on the calendar just talk to each other.

"Good morning!" She looks both full of life and exhausted.

"How are you feeling?" I ask her for a change.

"Pretty good this morning, thankfully."

"You look like you've got some energy. That's great!"

"Yea, I just hope I don't burn myself out too much today. We've got a lot to do."

"Take it easy for sure."

"How are you feeling, Madison? Are you in your car again?"

I let my body answer with surrender and indifference.

"Oh, Madison." I can already see the tears building—I just hope we end the call before she starts sobbing, again.

"It's fine, Ellie. This is expected."

She shakes her head. "No, it's not. I was never expected to watch my best friend die. Also, that trial..."

"I'm not doing the trial. It's not for me." I wave my hands in the air as I speak.

A few days ago, Ellie emailed a clinical trial for a new drug. I did a trial years ago, spending every weekend in the hospital running tests to see if a new treatment made a difference—it didn't.

"But, Madison, this one says..."

"No!" I cut her off, sternly.

"Ellie, has the detective called you again?"

"No. Oh and she didn't call the first time, she came up here to talk to me in person."

"Oh, interesting. She still hasn't tried contacting me, so I guess they figured out I didn't have anything to do with it at all. Whatever it is." I'm not sure if I'm trying to convince her or myself.

Ellie shrugs. "Yea, I guess. So weird."

We let it linger there, sharp and awkward.

"It's probably good you gave up ghost dating. You need to rest…" she doesn't finish her sentence.

"And die?" I finish it for her and she rolls her eyes.

"No."

"Ellie, I'm kidding. I mean I am dying but also I can joke about it." I know she doesn't think it's funny. "And actually, I took on one last client."

"Oh really?"

"Yea, I got a message from this woman named Lyn and it was just, I don't know, I just felt drawn to her. I want to help her. Or try."

Ugh, Madison, why are you doing this to yourself?

"Do you have the energy to?" *Good question.*

"Yea, it will only be a month or so. I told her I couldn't keep on for much more than that."

"That's good."

"How's the babies?" Of course her face lights up at the change to speak about her babies—just the distraction I needed.

"Well one is getting into everything and the other won't stop kicking me in my ribs."

"I can't wait to get up there to see them! And you of course!"

Ellie looks up, so they don't fill with tears. "Me either."

"I was actually thinking of coming up earlier than planned. Would that be okay?"

"Of course. When?"

"In a few weeks."

She claps her hands and I know I've just made her day a little brighter—even if it will be the last time I see her.

"What about this client?"

"Like I said, I should only be helping her about a month. And honestly, I can do this from anywhere."

"How long do you plan on staying?

"I'm not sure."

Unless, I die before I can get up there. I hope this is a promise I can keep though, I'd love to see my best friend—my sister—before I perish.

"Only, if that's okay with you?"

"Oh of course, Madison! You can stay as long as you want."

She needs to get on with her busy day, so we say our goodbyes.

LIAM AND JAMIE HAVE both continued the conversations with Lyn. I realized I didn't delete Liam's initial, disgusting message. My finger, now, hovers over the delete button.

Madison, just delete the message and move on. No more, you are helping Lyn find someone she can connect with. As the red delete button glares back at me, Liam messages again.

> So you coming to make me cum or what?

I let the air escape my mouth, loud, as I surrender. He's so repulsive.

Who does he think he is? What if he also hurts women?

Before I can think, screenshots of his profile have been uploaded to the Facebook group. Liam, like the other men, has a very strong internet presence—all it took was a reverse image search to find his full name, address, and phone number. I plug all relevant information in the people finder website.

I really do always hope I don't find anything bad, or disturbing about these men—so, I'm genuinely surprised when I find out all these awful things they have gotten away with.

Liam's criminal record is just as long as the other men's. Possession of illegal weapons, DUI, domestic violence, parole violation, assaulting a police officer, sexual assault. etc.

Where is our justice system? Why is this man free to just do as he pleases?

I double check arrest and jail records to make sure he isn't currently in prison—like he should be. I hear prisoners have been able to get phones and get on dating applications. Unfortunately, Liam is not currently in prison.

Oh big boy, I'm ready for you!

I SHOULDN'T BE HERE, doing this. The last time was the last time. Yet, here I am, sitting in my car, at a small park by the bayou waiting to meet Liam. After I posted his picture on Facebook, I messaged three women he victimized—I'm sure there are more out there.

They each had similar stories. He manipulated, cheated, gaslit, love bombed, and beat each of them. Two of them reported the violence and he spent a few months in jail, but basically just a slap on the wrist. One woman reported that he may have sexually abused her child—that sent me over the edge. I immediately messaged Liam to meet up. I was actually surprised when he agreed to meet at this park, instead of a bar. I was also surprised he wanted to meet so quickly.

There's still time to leave, Madison.

A black sedan pulls in next to me, a tall, thin man steps out of the car. Liam smiles at me in a friendly manner but looks around—he's expecting Lyn, but of course she isn't here. Five minutes pass, his frustration radiates, I finally get out of my car.

"Hey." I give a friendly wave, walking over to a bench.

"Hi," Liam strains nicety, looking past me—still expecting Lyn to show up. He then looks down at his phone in which he should see a text from Lyn, canceling.

"Damn," he says.

"Is everything okay?" I ask. Liam spins on his heels, almost losing his balance.

"Oh, yea. Just the person I was supposed to meet bailed." He sits on the bench to retie his shoes.

"Sucks. My friend just bailed on me too," I say.

He starts heading back to his car.

"Hey," I say, he turns back to look at me. "Want to just walk together? Since we both got stood up?"

He thinks for a minute. "Sure." He shrugs. "I'm Liam."

"Carrie." I grab two water bottles from my car, handing him one. "Here, I brought an extra bottle." He takes the water, but doesn't drink it immediately.

We make our way down to the bayou, in silence. Conversation finally starts flowing between us and I actually start enjoying Liam's company. He's a funny guy; briefly I forget all the horrible things he has done to others.

"Wow, we have already walked two miles," Liam says, looking down at his watch. He finishes the water in his bottle.

"Here, it's hot!" I hand him my water too. I packed them both full of drugs, just in case. I'm not sure if he noticed I haven't even touched mine; he didn't say anything if he did.

Liam misses his step as he tries grabbing the water bottle.

"You okay?" A faint smile tugs at my mouth.

His words slur, but he manages to get out, "I'm Detective Liam Callahan," before falling to the ground.

I pause. *Is this real? Detective?* No, he is Liam Brown a criminal, an abuser, pure evil.

"Madison Anderson." Two strangers dressed in black reveal themselves—where did they come from?

"Madison Anderson, I'm Detective Grace Oliver. Put your hands where I can see them and don't move."

I hesitate, but only for a second before I turn the opposite direction, sprinting away as fast as my frail body will take me. I've just got to get away from this bayou, away from the cops, away from my crimes.

I hear behind me, "Shit, Madison, you don't want to do this."

351

Detective Oliver

"Shit. Madison, you don't want to do this. Stay here with him and call for an ambulance."

I leave Liam crumbled on the sidewalk of the bayou—he should be fine, once the drugs leave his system, they aren't deadly just impairing.

"Detective? What? No." The officer protests.

"I don't have time to argue. Stay here." My jaw tightens. The officer we brought to help does as he's told.

I look out over the emptiness, *where could she have run to?*

"Ambulance two minutes out," my radio crackles as I start jogging down the path Madison took off down.

Evening shifts into night quicker than a match burns out in the wind. I avoid the urge to grab for my flashlight. Madison couldn't have gotten far, but I don't want her knowing when I am coming.

I come up on a set of stairs, glancing up at them—*did she run up?* I would have, if I were her trying to get away. Before I could take the first stair, I hear footsteps. I draw my gun and finally turn on my flashlight.

"Detective Oliver, Madison, is that you? Show yourself." I move around the stairs where the bayou curves.

A thin, pale woman walks around with her hands up, shaking, tears glimmering in the light.

"Please don't shoot," she pleads.

How is this the person responsible for murdering multiple men twice her size? We stare at each other—my gun still pointing at her face.

"Madison Lily Anderson?" She nods. "You are under arrest." I put my gun back on my hip, and go to grab her arm.

"Please don't do this." She pleads again. "You don't understand."

"I do, Madison. You murdered multiple men." I pause.

"Well, yes." She admits and shock washes over my face—criminals normally do not admit to their crimes.

My legs suddenly lead, frozen in place. "Why?"

"You have to know why Detective. If you were able to link me to them, you were able to figure out why. These men," she chokes. "They were horrible. They did horrible things."

"That doesn't make you killing them, okay. You have to understand that, right?"

She nods. "I know. But someone had to stop them."

"Yes, that's my job."

"Well, you haven't been doing a good job then." I sigh, she continues. "Sorry. I don't know if you had anything to do with their cases. But the police did nothing. The justice system did nothing. Women were beaten, raped, taken advantages of, kids were beaten and raped too."

I know all the details—I know all the crimes Madison thought she was righting. Our system failed those women; it's failed too many women, too many times. She reads this all over my face.

"You understand." It's almost a question, but she says it as a statement.

A breath slips out of me. "I do. I know the system failed. It failed you too, huh, Madison?"

She lowers her head.

"It failed me too," I say; she looks back at me surprised. I nod. "That's why I got into this particular line of business."

"What happened?" She asks in almost a whisper.

"I was raped. In high school. I did everything I was supposed to after, too. Went straight to the hospital, turned over my phone that incriminated the guy. They still let him go with less than a slap on the wrist." I take a deep breath—I don't relive that time in my life often and now I have several times in the last few weeks.

"My best friend's boyfriend. They said I begged for it and was drunk, so clearly it wasn't rape. I lost my friends, people didn't trust me, I thought my life was over."

"Look, Detective, I'm sorry that happened to you. Really I am so sorry. But it just means you really understand though. Didn't you just want to kill him after that?"

I did, I really did want to kill him, especially after no one believed me. I was taken advantage of, I was a victim, and no one listened to me. Meanwhile, they praised him, cheered him on. He helped win the championship football game for our school—how could he be a bad guy too?

"I really do understand."

I try to take a step closer to her, she takes a step back.

"But they were still people. People with families."

"Yea, so were all the women they hurt. All the women they changed."

I feel like I've been punched in the gut. I wonder just how much lives were changed, effected, because these men decided to do what they did. I know that I wouldn't be where I am in life if what happened to me didn't happen, but I always wish it never happened to me. I would never wish it one anyone else either. Madison has a point.

"It wasn't random." She begins to cry. "I didn't just kill random men off the street."

"I know, Madison. You believe you were protecting other women from these men."

She interrupts me. "Exactly! And they would have kept doing bad things. They weren't ever going to stop."

I nod my head. I took an oath to uphold the law. To arrest people like Madison. But I'm frozen. For the first time in my career, I don't know the difference between right and wrong. *What is justice after all?*

"You're pregnant?" She looks at my hand rubbing my belly—again, I didn't even know I was doing it—it's become an instinct at this point. I nod.

"Are you having a boy or girl?"

"Girl." I smile, even though I am talking about my unborn child with a serial killer.

"What if someone did something horrible to her?"

Tears form at the edges of my eyes, now. She knew just what to say to get to me, but it's true. If anyone hurts my daughter in any way, they will never see the light of day again. There's no question about that. Does that mean I would kill them? Honestly, I can't say.

"I know you are sick, Madison." I say.

"Oh yea. That," She laughs, but not because it's funny. "Definitely dying."

"That's got be hard to deal with."

She shakes her head. "I've been dealing with death my whole life. I've accepted it. I don't have much more time."

I let that linger between us. Vigilante Madison is a dying woman.

"I can't do this anymore," She says.

"What? Do what?"

"Murder anyone. I was done. Honestly, I can't believe I did it in the first place. Sometimes, I don't believe I did it. That it was me." She's disassociated from her actions, a lot of criminals do this. "I just wanted to help women. And it turned into me becoming a monster. Someone I don't recognize anymore."

I listen, letting the words linger in the space we share.

"After Travis, I was done. I'm getting weaker, but also I can't continue to be that woman. That person, who murders others. Oh god. What have I done?!" Her voice trembles.

"How long do you have?"

"A few weeks." I already knew this. I wanted to hear it from her.

"What did you have planned for the next few weeks?"

"Ha. Planned. I didn't have much planned really. What does a dying person plan?" She laughs again. "I got rid of all my stuff. What I have left is in my car. I was just going to drive."

"Go see Ellie?" I ask.

"She doesn't know anything. She wasn't involved at all. Please don't get her involved anymore," she pleads for her best friend's safety and freedom, but doesn't answer my question.

"She loves you very much Madison. I know you don't have many people in your life who you believe do. But she does." Something in me shifts, a wave of protection almost knocks me off my feet.

"I know." She looks to the left, as if she is still planning her escape.

I nod my head that way. She looks at me confused.

"Go." I whisper.

"What?"

"Go. Now. Before I change my mind." She doesn't hesitate. She runs out of sight.

I stand there, taking another deep breath. *What have I just done?*

"What happened?" Liam asks, from his hospital bed. The beeping from the machines a low symphony, reminding us we are still alive.

"She got away." I shrug. "Ran. Couldn't catch up to her."

He mimics my shrug. "Just like that? She just got away?"

I nod. "I don't know what else to tell you, Liam."

"You were gone for quite some time? You know when I was lying half-dead on the ground."

I laugh at his comment. "Yea. I tried chasing her for a while. But I lost her."

Liam looks at me skeptical. "Well, we have a BOLO for her with a description of her car. Hopefully she didn't get too far."

I nod, but I don't agree. I hope she got rid of her car and got very far away. I hope she never hurts another human being again. And I hope her last few weeks are peaceful.

"Well, you got a lot of paperwork to go fill out." He teases.

"How you feeling?" I ask. "I can't believe you drank the water a serial killer gave you." I want to laugh again, but none of it's actually funny.

"Been better. Wish all this had been worth it. But I'll be fine." He sighs and sinks back in bed. "You know, she wasn't actually a bad person."

Detective Oliver

3 Weeks Later

"Good morning." Liam greets me with a smile and a coffee as my phone rings.

"Detective Oliver." The caller ID says it is Ellie, Madison's best friend—I thought we were done with each other.

"Hey, it's Ellie."

"How are you?"

"Oh. Uh. I just called to let you know Madison passed."

"Oh, I'm so sorry, Ellie."

"Yea. I just thought you should know." Click; she hangs up with nothing more.

I stare off into the distance, my phone still up to my ear. Madison Lily Anderson died. I have more questions for Ellie; like, where has Madison been these few weeks? And did she kill anyone else? Questions I don't have answers to and never will. Case closed. Finally.

We found her car abandoned along I-10, headed west; which isn't the way one would drive to get to Kentucky. All of her things, her ID, keys, phone, wallet, left right there on the side of the highway with no sign of Madison. Gone. Vanished. Disappeared. Ghosted.

"Oliver?" Liam looks at me, confused. "Everything okay?"

I pull the phone away from my ear, putting it in back in my pocket.

"Everything is fine. Now, let's figure out what happened to our John Doe." I say as he hands me the case file he's been pouring over all morning.

Acknowledgements

I started *Ghost Dater* two years ago after reentering the dating world following a long relationship and marriage. What I encountered, and what other women shared, made it impossible not to pay attention. The patterns were familiar. This book grew from the refusal to ignore them.

I wrote it to examine what we normalize, what we excuse, and what it costs us when we do. To sit with the discomfort rather than explain it away. And to explore what happens when women stop minimizing their instincts for the sake of peace.

Along the way, I was supported by people who believed in this story, and in me, even when I struggled to do either myself. To the friends and family who offered encouragement, patience, humor, and steady presence—thank you. You made the long stretches of doubt easier to move through.

This journey also introduced me to a broader community of writers, readers, and kind strangers met both in person and online. The conversations, shared understanidng, and generosity I encountered along the way mattered more than I can fully express. This book is better because of it.

To Bruce Wayne—thank you for believing in me long before I believed in myself, and for being a safe place to land while I brought this story into the world.

I am also grateful to everyone who helped shape this novel into what it is today—through thoughtful feedback, challenge, care, or conversation. Your influence lives quietly within these pages.

To the readers: thank you for choosing this book and for trusting me with your time. I hope you feel seen here.

And to the women who have endured some of the things written about in these pages—I see you. I am you. I love you. I hope you find safety, joy, and happiness.

And finally, I want to acknowledge myself. I have dreamed of writing and publishing a book since I was seven years old. I started *Ghost Dater*, committed to finishing it and chose to bring it into the world. I did it.

About the author

Brandi Autumn is a writer whose work examines power, protection, and the quiet dangers we learn to live with. *Ghost Dater* is her debut novel. She lives in Houston and is often found writing in coffee shops.